CRIME BITERS!

IT'S A DOGGY DOG WORLD

TOMMY GREENWALD
WITH ILLUSTRATIONS BY ADAM STOWER

WITHDRAWN

| SCHOLASTIC PRESS | NEW YORK

Library of Congress Cataloging-in-Publication Data available

ISBN 978-0-545-78397-2

10 9 8 7 6 5 4 3 2 1   16 17 18 19 20

Printed in the U.S.A.   23
First edition, October 2016

Book design by Yaffa Jaskoll

THIS BOOK IS DEDICATED TO ALL THE
PEOPLE WHO RESCUE ANIMALS . . .

AND TO ALL THE ANIMALS WHO
RESCUE PEOPLE.

AND A SPECIAL WAG OF THE TAIL TO
JENNIFER WORSFOLD, WHO COINED THE PHRASE
THAT INSPIRED THE TITLE OF THIS BOOK.

THE CRIMEBITERS OATH

We, the CrimeBiters,
pledge to serve society,
help our fellow human beings,
protect the community from crime,
defend each other against all enemies,
preserve our freedoms and rights,
and eat as much chocolate ice cream as possible.

Jimmy Bishop
Irwin Wonk
Daisy Flowers
Baxter Bratford

P.S. The CrimeBiters are the only ones who know my dog
Abby's secret (even though some of the other CrimeBiters
don't believe me).
(Okay, fine—ALL the other CrimeBiters.)

PROFILE UPDATE

Name: Jimmy Bishop

Age: 11

Occupation: President and Founder, CrimeBiters

Interests: Solving crime, protecting society, Daisy Flowers

INTRODUCTION

REMEMBER WHEN I TOLD YOU about the time I adopted this dog, Abby, and she turned out to be this awesome crime-fighting vampire dog, and together with my pals Irwin Wonk and Daisy Flowers we solved the biggest crime to hit Quietville in years, and then we made friends with Baxter Bratford, the ex-bully and son of the criminal mastermind Barnaby Bratford, and the four of us (plus Abby) formed the CrimeBiters?

Remember that?

That was so awesome.

If you don't remember, then you'll just have to trust me: Abby *does* have secret powers.

She fights crime. She can fly, under certain conditions.

She may well be a vampire.

You believe me, right?

Good. I'm glad.

Because nobody else did, at first.

But now people are starting to get it.

People are beginning to understand what we're dealing with here: one very special dog.

With extra emphasis on *special*.

PART ONE

GOOD DOG

"THIS MEETING OF THE CRIMEBITERS is called to order!" I announced.

Abby, Irwin, Daisy, and I had just gotten to the old abandoned Boathouse, which had become our clubhouse. After tying Abby to a big tree, where she quickly fell asleep (she sleeps a lot during the day, just like most vampires), the rest of us headed up to the roof, where we had our weekly meetings.

"Why do you always get to call the meeting to order?" Irwin asked.

Sometimes there was no point in answering Irwin, so I ignored him.

"Should we wait for Baxter?" Daisy asked. Baxter was the fourth member of our gang. "He's not here yet."

"What else is new?" Irwin grumbled. Irwin wasn't all that crazy about Baxter, because of who Baxter is. Or rather, who he used to be—a bully who made me and Irwin miserable. Also, he happens to be the son of Barnaby Bratford—the same Barnaby Bratford who was stealing jewelry from people all over town, until Abby, Daisy, Irwin, and I all helped catch him.

So why did we invite his son the ex-bully to join the CrimeBiters?

I guess the only answer is: It's a long story.

FACT: Everything you ever wanted to know about the Barnaby Bratford crime ring is in the first CrimeBiters book. It's a really good book. And I'm not just saying that because I'm in it.

"Baxter told me he'd be a little late," I said. "We can start without him. Let's begin with our criminal reports in and around the Quietville area. Daisy, please give us your update."

Daisy stood up and took out a piece of paper.

"Case file for the week," she announced. "Friday: While at the beach, I observed Mrs. Knofla putting down a cooler to reserve a picnic table and then leaving the area, which is strictly against town rules."

PROFILE UPDATE

Name: Daisy Flowers

Age: Just turned 11

Occupation: Cofounder of the CrimeBiters

Interests: Amazingly enough, wanting to hang around with us

"Did you tell the beach patrol?" Irwin asked.

"I wanted to," Daisy said, "but my mom wouldn't let me. She said people do it all the time, including her."

"Oh," Irwin said.

Daisy continued, "Tuesday: I observed four incidents of cell phone usage while driving. I advised the local traffic officer, who assured me he would keep a lookout for any further illegal activity of that kind." She folded up her piece of paper. "That's all for now."

"Thank you for that excellent update, Daisy," I said. "Quietville is a safer place because of your dedication."

"Quietville is a safer place because nothing ever happens around here," Irwin mumbled.

"That's not true," I told him.

Irwin rolled his eyes. "Why do think it's called Quietville?"

I rolled my eyes right back. "I don't know! Now, do you have a report or not?"

He stood up. "Yeah. Uh, I didn't observe any suspicious activity this week."

"Seriously?" Daisy asked. "Not one thing?"

"Nope." Irwin shuffled his feet. "But I'm happy to report that my mom said our sweatshirts will be ready in two weeks."

"Sweet!" I said. Irwin and I high-fived. Team uniforms! This was a big moment in the life of our club. The sweatshirts looked so cool—they were blue and gold, had Abby's picture on the front, and on the back it said CRIMEBITERS: SINKING OUR TEETH INTO BAD GUYS SINCE 2015.

A voice came from downstairs. "Hey, everybody!" Baxter was making his way up to the roof. "Sorry I'm late. Lacrosse practice."

"So, what's the deal with lacrosse?" Irwin asked. "Are you going to have to go to practice a lot?"

"I don't know, maybe," Baxter said, self-consciously fiddling with his shirt collar. "The season only started a few weeks ago. Why?"

Irwin harumphed. "I just want to know if it's going to interfere with our meetings."

"But I love lacrosse," Baxter said.

"More than the gang?" Irwin challenged him.

"Stop it, Irwin," Daisy said. "It's great that Baxter plays lacrosse, because it helps him forget about what happened with his dad."

"Whatever," mumbled Irwin. The more Daisy stuck up for Baxter, the more annoyed Irwin got. "Sports are stupid anyway."

"They are not," Daisy said. "Sports are great."

PROFILE UPDATE

Name: Irwin Wonk

Age: 11

Occupation: Best Friend and Cofounder of the CrimeBiters

Interests: Questioning everything I do

PROFILE UPDATE

Name: Baxter Bratford

Age: 12

Occupation: CrimeBiter

Interests: Trying to make everyone forget he used to be a bully

"My parents have been trying to get me to play a sport," I blurted out, wanting to participate in the conversation. This was only half-true. They had mentioned it once, but after I stopped laughing, they didn't bring it up again.

But that was before Daisy announced that sports were great.

"No, seriously," I added. "They have."

The others all looked at me. Me taking up a sport was kind of like an elephant taking up tap dancing.

"Why?" Irwin asked sensibly.

"Because it will make me more well-rounded," I said. "And they want me to get more exercise."

Abby suddenly woke up and started barking her head off at a chipmunk that was getting too close. She would have chased her to the next county too, if not for the leash I had tied around the tree.

"Even Abby thinks you playing a sport is a crazy idea," Daisy said, giggling.

"Ha-ha-ha-ha!" Irwin said, laughing way too loudly at Daisy's joke.

"Well, I already decided," I said, annoyed. "I'm joining the lacrosse team with Baxter." I hadn't decided anything of the sort, of course, until that very second.

"Cool!" Baxter said. "The season already started, but maybe they'll let you join! Next practice is tomorrow."

"Wait, what?" I said. Tomorrow was really soon. The soonest possible day, in fact.

"I'm sorry for laughing," Daisy said. "I think it's awesome. I promise to come to all your games."

The idea of Daisy watching me flounder around on the lacrosse field suddenly filled me with dread. I desperately searched for a way to take it all back, but couldn't come up with anything.

"Do you have a report for us, Baxter?" I asked finally.

"I definitely do!" He sat down. "Yesterday, I was walking home from school when I saw a man get out of a car, take off all of his clothes except his underwear, run into some guy's yard, jump in the pool, splash around, and yell, 'I LOVE PIE! I LOVE PIE!' and then run back to his car and drive away."

Oooh. This sounded exciting. "Did you report it?" I asked.

Baxter nodded. "I was going to, but the guy in the car turned out to be your father." He broke into a giant grin. "NAILED YA!"

"I hate you!" I screamed, then jumped on him and wrestled him to the ground. We were both laughing, of course. One of our CrimeBiters traditions was to make up the most ridiculous crimes we could think of, and then say that someone's family member did it. If anyone ever fell for it—like I just did—they had to bring the snacks for the next meeting.

"I'll take Yodels and Yoo-hoo," Baxter gasped, between wrestles.

"Those are the unhealthiest snacks ever," Daisy said.

Baxter and I got to our feet. "That concludes our official club business for today," I panted, still out of breath. "Does anyone want to play tag before we go?"

"I can't," Irwin said. "I gotta get home."

"Already?" I moaned. He had a really strict mom. My mom was really strict too, but she wasn't home that much. My dad was home a lot, but he wasn't strict at all.

"Yup, already. I have a cello lesson." Irwin stood up. "Daisy, do you want to walk home with me?"

Well, I certainly wasn't going to let that happen without me. "Fine, I'll walk home with you guys too."

"You can't," Irwin said quickly. "Your mom is picking you up, remember?"

"Oh yeah," I said. We were taking our monthly trip to the farmer's market. "So hold on—you guys are just going to walk home without me?"

"What do you want us to do, sleep here?" Irwin said, with a little twinkle in his eyes.

"Fine," I said glumly.

Baxter rolled his eyes. He was pretty tired of Irwin and me fighting over Daisy all the time. Not that I blamed him.

FACT: Irwin has a major crush on Daisy.

ANOTHER FACT: So do I.

AND YET ANOTHER FACT: Daisy says it's best if we're all "just friends," so things don't get too complicated.

THE LAST AND SADDEST FACT: She's absolutely right.

I untied Abby from the tree and we all formed a circle, put our hands into the middle, and yelled what we yelled at the end of every meeting.

"CRIMEBITERS FOREVER!"

"See you guys later," Daisy said, and she and Irwin

headed down the hill. As I waved good-bye, I tried not to feel too jealous of their walk home. I tried to convince myself that no matter what, we were a gang, and we were going to stick together. And overall, it had been a pretty good meeting. I was just starting to feel better when Baxter had to go and ruin it.

"Welcome to the lacrosse team!" he said.

CHAPTER 2

HAVE YOU EVER BEEN TO A FARMER'S MARKET?

It's basically a bunch of people walking around the parking lot of some school, pretending it's 1857 and we're all in a giant field somewhere. Meanwhile, almost everyone there is trying to sell you something that tastes terrible: carrots, cabbage, tomatoes, celery, brussels sprouts, and more gross stuff like that. There are also people who sell various kinds of melons and berries. Fruit is okay, I guess, if there's nothing else to eat.

There are two reasons, though, that I don't mind going to the farmer's market with my mom: One is that Abby gets to come, since it's outside; and two is that there's a big, bearded guy in overalls named Isaac who sells the best chocolate chip cookies I've ever tasted. Whenever we go there, we stop at Isaac's booth first, and he usually slips me a few extra cookies on the side.

"Only one cookie today," my mom said as we got out of the car. She had her phone in her hand, as usual. She was pretty attached to her phone, even on weekends.

"Isaac!" I said, running up to him.

"Jimmy, my boy!" Isaac was grinning. "Had enough of those fruits and veggies?"

"Ew!" I cried.

He bent down to pet Abby. "Who's a good girl?" he said. "How are you today? Hungry as usual?" Abby stared up at him and yawned. Isaac whistled, looking at her enormous fangs. "Wouldn't want to be on the wrong end of those babies, that's for sure."

FACT: Abby has the biggest fangs in America.

My mom shook hands with Isaac. "Actually, we'll get a few cookies for dessert. Maybe half a dozen?"

"Sounds great," Isaac said.

He went to pick out the chocolatiest, chippiest ones, while my mom turned back to me. "So, is this lacrosse thing for real?" On the way there I'd told her about my conversation with the rest of the gang, and she'd nearly driven off the road.

"Yeah, it's for real, whether I like it or not," I said. "Daisy already promised she'd come to all the games."

My mom laughed. "Well, in that case!"

Suddenly I felt a YANK!

My whole arm jerked forward. Abby started pulling on her leash so hard that I could feel it down to my toes.

"Abby!" I cried. "Settle down!"

But she had no interest in settling down. In fact, she unsettled up.

YANK! PULL! YANK! OUCH! YANK!

On the fourth YANK! I couldn't take it anymore. I dropped the leash, and Abby was off and running, with me right behind her, and my mom right behind me.

"I'll hold the cookies for you!" called Isaac.

Through the kale stand, past the broccoli station, under the bread booth (the only other good stop in the whole place), over the beans display, and around the corner near the spinach section, Abby dashed and darted, knocking food onto the ground and making people drop their precious vegetables.

FACT: There's actually no such thing as precious vegetables.

PROFILE UPDATE

Name: Sarah Bishop

Age: That's private information she refuses to give out.

Occupation: Something that involves nice clothes and a briefcase

Interests: Telling my dad that he's too easy on me

"Jimmy, catch her!" hollered my mom. "For crying out loud!"

"I'm trying!"

"Well, try harder!"

Finally Abby saw what she was looking for.

Out came the fangs.

"Uh-oh," I said out loud, even though no one was listening.

I lunged for her, but I was too late. Abby launched herself up into the air, then landed on what looked like a perfectly nice lady, who was minding her own business, squeezing some melons to make sure they were ripe.

"GRRRRR!" said Abby to the lady, throwing in a little fang just for fun.

"ABBY, NO!" That was my mother, who had a look of pure horror on her face.

The woman who'd been Abby's target was too shocked to say anything. She just screamed, "AAAARRGGHHH!" and threw her pocketbook up into the air.

Out of the pocketbook fell four extremely scrumptious-looking peanut-butter cookies.

Abby quickly lost interest in the woman and ate two of the cookies.

"ABBY!" I yelled.

"ABBY!" my mom yelled louder.

But Abby just looked at us and kept chomping away.

FACT: To a dog, a delicious snack is worth a few humans yelling at you.

As everyone gathered around to help the poor woman, I picked up her pocketbook and the other two cookies to give them back. But before I could, I felt a hand on my shoulder.

21

I looked up to see Isaac standing there. "Where did you get those?" he asked, pointing at the cookies.

"They were the lady's," I explained. "Abby ate two already."

Isaac nodded slowly. "This explains everything."

I scratched my head. "Huh?"

But Isaac wasn't paying attention to me anymore. He marched over to the woman. "I have seen you at my cookie stand often, but you never buy anything. Meanwhile, I've noticed that my inventory has not been matching my income." He pointed at her with one of his long fingers. "Have you been stealing my cookies?"

The lady, who had been straightening out her clothes, looked completely offended. "Well, I never! First I am attacked by this dreadful animal, and now this!"

"It seems quite clear to me," Isaac said, "that you are a thief."

As everyone began murmuring about the possibility that there was a criminal in our midst, I quietly picked up Abby, who was still licking crumbs off her lips.

Another woman who sold yogurt-on-a-stick (yuck!) came over. "There's a simple way to figure this out. Ma'am, do you have a receipt for your purchase?"

"Who gets receipts at a farmer's market?" the

lady snapped. "That's enough of this nonsense, I'm leaving!"

She tried to grab her purse out of my hand, but for some reason I held on to it. She pulled again, harder. I pulled back, just as hard. Suddenly, in the middle of this purse tug-of-war, something long and green fell out.

A cucumber.

The lady went white. "What—I have no idea how that got in there! I was just about to pay for it, I swear!"

I couldn't believe it! Not the part about her being a thief—that was totally believable. But stealing a *cucumber*? Who does that?

Big, bearded Isaac walked up to her. "Ma'am? We don't want to make a big deal out of this. You are free to go." He slowly, gently put his hand on her shoulder. "But if you ever come back to our market again, we will be forced to call the police."

Without another word, the lady grabbed her purse and ran.

Isaac bent down and scratched Abby's head. "She works hard for her cookies, eh?"

"I guess so," I said.

What I was actually thinking was:

She works hard to fight crime.

CHAPTER 3

"HOLD ON A SEC," said my dad. "You think Abby chased some lady clear across the farmer's market because she knew the lady was a thief?" It was later that night, and we were just sitting down to dinner. My dad looked at me like he wanted to believe me, but just couldn't bring himself to do it.

"That's *exactly* what I'm saying," I answered. "I mean, yeah, she was perfectly happy to eat the cookies once she got there, but somehow she knew what that lady was up to."

My dad laughed. "Okay, Jimmy. Whatever you say."

Misty, my older sister, helped herself to a piece of chicken, which wasn't easy, considering she was also texting and scrolling through her music at the same time.

PROFILE UPDATE

Name: Misty Bishop

Age: That really obnoxious age where everything she does is annoying (which is pretty much any age, by the way)

Occupation: Sister, Buyer of Stuff

Interests: Her phone, her boyfriend Jarrod

FACT: It's amazing what a person can do with one hand, as long as that hand is attached to a phone.

"Jimmy!" she said, really loudly since she had headphones on. "I just got a text from Jarrod. He says Baxter told Chad that you're joining the lacrosse team?" Jarrod Knight was Misty's boyfriend, and Chad was Jarrod's little brother.

"Yeah, I am," I confirmed. "First practice is tomorrow."

"Isn't it awesome?" my dad said, beaming.

Misty snorted. "Just don't get yourself killed."

"I won't," I said, trying to snort back.

Suddenly there was a scream from the front door.

"NOOOOOOO!!!!"

That was my mom, who'd just gotten home from yoga.

We heard it again: "NOOOOOOO!!!!"

The three of us at the kitchen table looked at one another.

"Uh-oh," said my dad.

My first thought was to look down to see if Abby was under the table, where she usually hangs out during dinner. She wasn't.

"Double uh-oh," I said.

Sure enough, two seconds later Abby came flying into the room with something in her mouth. Five seconds after that, my mom came flying in after her.

"STOP THAT DOG!" she screamed.

I immediately saw what the problem was. Abby, who was having a blast by the way, had something in her mouth.

Something off limits.

Something expensive.

Something that my mom wanted very, very much.

FACT: What dogs consider toys are often, as it turns out, the opposite of toys.

"GET THAT SHOE AWAY FROM HER!" my mom hollered.

I dove under the table, grabbed Abby, and started pulling at the shoe. To Abby, of course, this was all part of the game. She refused to let go. She growled playfully and dug in her fangs. I pulled. She pulled. It was kind of like me and that lady at the farmer's market—but this time, Abby was the thief.

Then she gave one last big pull, and I heard an upsetting sound.

RIIIIIPPPPP!

The shoe came apart like it was made of tissue paper. (For all I know, it was. Really expensive tissue paper.) Abby looked at the destroyed shoe, decided it wasn't a toy worth enjoying anymore, gave me a *no hard feelings* lick on the nose, and immediately went to take a snooze on the couch.

My parents looked at me.

"What?" I said. "Mom's the one who left her shoes in the hall!"

My mom didn't respond. She just bent down, picked up the shoe, and put it on the kitchen table. It looked like it had been stomped on and chewed up by ten wild cougars.

"This is the third pair of my shoes Abby has destroyed this month alone," she said, her voice barely above a whisper. I shuddered inside. It's when she talks softly that you really have to worry.

"And she also ruined my favorite pair of slippers, and last night she slurped all over my phone," Misty added. "For a minute I thought the battery was ruined!"

I glared at my sister.

"Hey, you know what?" I announced. "I'm actually not that hungry. I think I'm going to go watch a little *STOP! POLICE!*" *STOP! POLICE!* was an old TV show about a cop named Hank Barlow, and it was my favorite show ever. But at that moment, I was pretty sure I wasn't going to make it into the den to watch my old buddy Hank.

My mom spoke first. "Actually, Jimmy, no television right now."

"Take a seat," said my dad, sighing.

"We need to talk," began my mom.

"About what?" I asked, as if I didn't know.

She pointed at the shoe. "You don't even want to know how much these cost." She was right, I didn't. "And after what happened at the farmer's market . . ."

"She caught a thief at the market!" I protested.

"That was luck," my mom said. "You and I both know Abby just wanted those cookies."

"Who says?"

"I say!"

"Okay, that's enough," my dad butted in, a little less excitedly. He didn't get nearly as upset about Abby's powers of destruction. Maybe because the stuff she usually destroyed was Mom's.

"I'm really sorry," I said, "and I know Abby is sorry too. It won't happen again."

My mom laughed, but not because she thought anything was funny. "Well, that's just the thing, Jimmy. It will happen again. And again and again and again, unless we do something about it."

Right at that moment, Abby got up from the couch, jumped up onto my lap, and curled up like the cutest, sweetest, most innocent little dog in the whole world.

PROFILE UPDATE

Name: Richard Bishop

Age: I forget exactly

Occupation: Consultant (which I think is code for "doesn't have a full-time job")

Interests: Making sure everyone in the family gets along

FACT: Dogs know when they're in trouble, which is when they play the "adorable" card. Can you blame them?

I looked at my mom hopefully. But sadly, she wasn't fooled for a second.

"You can't make me give her up!" I insisted. "Remember, you promised! And after everything she's done for us!" Which included a lot of stuff, like for instance practically saving my life.

"No one's talking about giving Abby up," said my dad. "Calm down."

I was confused. "Well, what then?"

"Dad and I have actually been talking about this," said my mom, "and we think we have an answer."

I waited.

"Obedience training," said my dad.

"What's that?"

"It's like a class," he said, reaching over to pet Abby. "We'll go to a dog trainer who can teach Abby how to behave, obey, and listen."

"How to not destroy the house and everything in it," my mom added.

I thought for a second. That didn't sound so terrible.

"If that doesn't work," my dad said, "we may need to try something else, like putting a muzzle on her."

"A muzzle? You mean over her mouth?" That *did* sound terrible.

"No one *wants* to put a muzzle on her," said my mom. "But she can't just keep treating all my belongings as her personal toy collection. Not to mention the fact that she's either bitten or almost bitten several people."

"Several *bad* people!" I corrected.

My dad sighed. "We don't really know that for sure, do we?" He patted me on the back in a *sorry son, but it's settled* kind of way. "We'll do the training first, and see how it goes."

I decided that nothing good could happen from continuing this conversation. "Okay, fine. Can I get some dessert and go watch TV?"

My dad nodded. He was much happier giving me large bowls of ice cream than talking about a tricky subject. But my mom wasn't done.

"Also, we need to talk about this lacrosse thing," she said. "If you're really serious about it, Dad needs to pick you up after school to buy the equipment."

FACT: Sports that require equipment should generally be avoided.

"I think it's great," said my dad. "I'm impressed that this was your idea, Jimmy."

"Actually, maybe I should think about it for a little while first," I said. "Not jump into anything. I mean, the season's already started and everything."

"Oh, come on!" my mom said. "Organized activities are terrific, and lacrosse is a wonderful sport."

Now *that* was funny, because if there were two words I'd never ever heard her say, they were *La* and *Crosse*.

I tried to take advantage of the situation. "Okay, fine. But since I'm being such a great guy and taking up a sport, will you guys promise to never put a muzzle on Abby as long as we live?"

My mom, who was tired of always being the bad guy, looked at my dad.

"I bought some Rocky Road for dessert," he said.

CHAPTER 4

AFTER DINNER—I GOTTA ADMIT, that ice cream definitely did hit the spot—I watched a few episodes of *STOP! POLICE!* on my computer. Then I headed up to my room to read *Fangs a Million,* one of my favorite Jonah Forrester books. Jonah, in case you've been living under a rock, is only the coolest vampire of all time, in my personal opinion. He's a noble vampire and only uses his powers to help society—kind of like Abby. In *Fangs a Million,* though, Jonah suddenly inherits a million dollars from a mysterious relative, and becomes rich and lazy. Then he finds out that the mysterious relative was the head of a crime gang trying to take over all of California, and was just trying to tempt Jonah into giving up his vampire ways. It's super intense. I've read the book at least six times.

By ten o'clock, I was on chapter twelve. I heard a *whoosh!* and I looked up.

Abby was creeping out my bedroom window.

She goes out the same window almost every night. Back when she first started doing it, I tried to spy on her and follow her to see where she went, but then I realized that as a vampire dog, she needed privacy to do her job.

Also, I'm not all that crazy about the dark.

That night, I heard her growling. I peered out the window and saw her working hard on a hole, trying to get to Herman. Herman was the name I'd given the groundhog that lived under our yard, who was probably just trying to mind his own business before bed.

"Abby!" I hissed. "No digging! Leave poor Herman alone!"

She looked up.

"Come to bed!" I called. "I appreciate the effort, but like I keep saying, animals aren't bad guys. Herman is actually a very nice groundhog."

Abby stared down at the hole, then back up at me. It seemed like she was trying to decide what to do.

Then she waved at me with her tail and kept digging.

I lay down in bed, letting Abby do her thing. I had no idea what that was. I just knew that she was always back in my closet, sleeping on my clothes, by the time I woke up the next morning.

"Night, Abby," I called out to her. "Say hi to Herman for me."

All I heard in response was panting, digging, and the wind pushing the branches into the side of the house.

CHAPTER 5

"I CAN'T BELIEVE YOU CAME!" Baxter exclaimed when I showed up at lacrosse practice the next day.

"Yup," I said.

Baxter laughed before he could stop himself. "Ha! Oh, uh, no offense or anything, Jimmy, but I thought you were saying all that stuff just to impress Daisy."

I was, I thought.

"I'm so glad Jimmy's joining the team," my dad said to Baxter. "You two are gonna crush it!"

"Easy, dad," I said, glaring at him—ever since this whole lacrosse thing came up, he'd been acting like I was a combination of Tom Brady and LeBron James.

My dad was holding all the lacrosse equipment we'd just bought. "You ready to put this stuff on?"

I nodded glumly. When I'd tried it all on at the store, I didn't even recognize myself in the mirror. I still didn't.

"How does it feel?" my dad asked, as I pulled on the pads.

"Like I'm going to war," I answered.

"Let me see your stick," Baxter said. I handed it to him, and he examined it. "You realize this is a goalie stick, right? How did you know we needed a goalie? Our last one just got hurt when the goal post fell on him. Never seen that before."

Oh, terrific. "All I know is the guy at the store said you don't have to worry as much about skills and speed and all that stuff if you play goalie."

Baxter whistled. "Yeah, but you have to worry about a hard ball speeding straight for your head," he said.

"Wait, what?" I said, alarmed. "How hard?"

Before Baxter had a chance to answer, though, somebody blew a sharp whistle directly behind my left eardrum.

"CIRCLE UP!" a voice yelled.

I turned around to see a bunch of kids running straight at me. "Hey, watch out!" I screamed, but they all ran past me and lined up in front of the man who'd yelled. He wore dark sunglasses, had the biggest jaw I'd ever seen, and looked like he was born with that whistle in his mouth.

"Boys, let's focus!" the guy barked. "If we're going to take this championship from those LaxMax bums, we've got to stay sharp!"

"Who's LaxMax?" I whispered to Baxter.

"The best team in the league," he whispered back. "They've been undefeated forever. And they've beaten us in the finals two straight years. Coach can't stand them."

"Start your stretches!" the coach commanded. "We've got a lot of work to do!" Then he walked over to me and my dad. "You must be Jimmy," he said, sticking out his hand. "I'm Coach Knight."

I shook his hand. "Are you Chad's dad?"

"I sure am," said Mr. Knight. "Are you two friends?"

"Kind of, I guess. My sister goes out with your son Jarrod."

"Oh, right," Mr. Knight said. "Well, no time for chit-chat now. It's time to play ball!"

"Great," I said, because I was worried that if I didn't, the coach might eat me. He seemed super intense.

Coach shook hands with my dad. "We don't get a lot of boys joining the team midseason but I'm sure your son will be just fine," he said. "Team sports are terrific for a child's development."

PROFILE

Name: Coach Knight

Age: Around my dad's age, I think

Occupation: Coach of the lacrosse team

Interests: His whistle

"I couldn't agree more," said my dad.

Coach Knight noticed my dad wasn't showing any sign of leaving. "Terrific. Well, I've got it from here," he added.

"Right!" My dad laughed, and then headed to the car.

As my dad walked away, Coach elbowed me. "Parents," he said. "They can be tougher than the opponents, am I right?"

"Yes, sir."

"You don't have to call me sir. Call me Coach."

"Yes, sir. I mean Coach."

I glanced over and saw Chad Knight warming up. He was in my grade at school, but the only thing he'd ever said to me was "Are you in line?" and the only thing I'd ever said to him was "No, you can go ahead of me," even though I had definitely been in line at the time.

FACT: There are two kinds of people in the world. Athletes, and people who get in the way of athletes.

"Chad is amazing at sports," I'd told my dad on the ride to practice. "Like, the best in our school."

"That's nice," said my dad. I knew what he was thinking: *I sure hope my son turns out to be amazing at sports too*. It wasn't going to be fun disappointing him. Wasn't it enough that I was amazing at watching old TV shows on the computer?

"So, Jimmy!" Mr. Knight whacked me on the back, which kind of hurt a little. "You really want to give goalie a try?"

"Uh, sure."

"Terrific! It just so happens we need a goalie, since our last one, Jonny Galt, got injured last game." He shook his head. "Freak accident. No wonder he decided to quit and join the Quietville Bagpiping Club. I didn't even know we had that here. Anyway, throw that helmet on, grab your stick, and come with me!"

I did as I was told and followed the coach. My dad, who was standing by the car trying to make himself leave, gave me a thumbs-up. I grimly waved back.

Coach Knight took me over to the goal, told me to stand in front of it, and then started tossing the lacrosse ball at me, really softly. I caught every one. *This isn't so bad*, I said to myself.

"Let's try one a tiny bit harder," said Mr. Knight, and he backed up about ten feet. Then he wound up and took a shot. The ball looked like a big white bullet as it whistled its way toward my face.

"ARRRGGGH!" I screamed. I put up my hands, as much for self-defense as anything else.

PLUNK! The ball nestled comfortably right in the netting of my stick. I stared at it in disbelief.

"Nice save!" Mr. Knight came jogging up with a big grin on his face. "Hey, boys!" he hollered at the rest of the team. "Looks like we found ourselves a goalie!" He turned to me. "Well done, son," he said, giving me another whack on the back.

This time, it didn't hurt at all.

CHAPTER 6

I HADN'T BEEN BACK to the Northport Animal Rescue Foundation (otherwise known as Northport ARF!) since the day we adopted Abby, but it was like I'd never been away.

As soon as my dad and I walked in that night, all the dogs started wagging and woofing in their cages, begging me to say hello. Abby, meanwhile, was walking around like she owned the place, greeting everyone like a long-lost friend. The staff was really happy to see her, because they love it when one of the rescues winds up in a good home.

"She thinks she's the mayor," said my dad.

I nodded. "She kind of is."

We were trying to figure out where the obedience training class met when I heard a voice behind us.

"There she is!"

I turned and saw someone walking toward us, and realized it was the guy who first pulled Abby out of the cage for us when we picked her out.

"Hey!" I said.

My dad shook his hand. "Good to see you again," he said, and I realized neither of us knew the guy's name.

"I'm Shep," he said, helping us out.

Shep looked at me closely. "Yo, dude, no offense or anything, but didn't you used to have . . . like . . . a thing on your face?"

I touched my cheek. "Oh, yeah," I said. "That was gross. It's gone now." Shep was asking about my blotch, which was this weird rash that popped up on my face right before the first day of school. Luckily it went away, after my mom got me some medicine and after I made some friends. I think both helped.

My dad laughed. "Hey, Shep, remember when I picked Abby up for the first time, and she sneezed on me?"

Shep chuckled. "I sure do, man. But you took her any-way, which I gotta say was pretty impressive." He bent down to pet Abby. "So how's my little girl doing? Still sleeping the day away?"

"Yup!" I said. "She's awesome! She likes to sleep or

PROFILE

Name: Shep

Age: As old as you have to be to have long gray hair and a long white mustache

Occupation: The best job in the world—dog shelter guy

Interests: Why would he need any? He's the dog shelter guy.

hide under the porch during the day, and at night she gets really active, and she helped catch a jewelry thief a few months ago, and she helped catch a cookie thief a few days ago, and she hates garlic and has enormous fangs and goes through the window every night—"

"Whoa, slow down there, chief," Shep said. He looked down at Abby fondly. "I do remember she was quite a character, back when we had her. Has a lot of interesting habits, that's for sure."

"And also a lot of naughty ones," added my dad. "Which is why we're here."

"I get that," Shep said, nuzzling Abby's ear. Abby purred with happiness. (Hey, dogs can purr too, you know.)

FACT: If you want a dog to like you, scratch her ear. If you want a dog to love you, give her food. If you want a dog to worship the ground you walk on, give her food while scratching her ear.

"You guys ready to get started?" Shep said. "The rest of the class is already outside."

"Actually, I'm not staying," my dad said. "I need to go pick up my daughter. I hope that's okay?"

Shep frowned for a second. "Oh, yeah, no problem-o. Well, for sure, it's not all that common for a child to go through dog obedience training without an adult present, but if it's all good with you, then it's all good with me."

"It's all good with me," my dad said, who looked like he was trying to figure out if Shep was the coolest guy he'd ever met, or someone he shouldn't necessarily be leaving his son with. "Jimmy can handle it, and I'll be back to pick him up in an hour," my dad said. "Abby is his dog, and they're great with each other."

I beamed. "Thanks, Dad."

"It's other things she needs to work on," he added.

"Meaning what, exactly?" asked Shep.

"Meaning, she chews up everything in the house, she wanders the neighborhood at night, she growls at people sometimes—"

"Only bad people," I interrupted.

My dad sighed. "Well, you wouldn't want to be on the wrong end of those fangs, is all I'm saying."

"We can work on all of that, except the fangs," Shep said. He bent over and petted Abby, who was starting to look a little bored. "I'm going to take this cute little girl out to the yard with the other trainees. We'll get started in a minute."

Shep started to leave with Abby, then turned back.

"Inside every dog is a sweetheart just waiting to come out," he said. "Sooner or later, they all come around."

My dad sighed. "Sooner would be good."

CHAPTER 7

THE OBEDIENCE TRAINING took place in a large circle in the yard behind the shelter. It looked kind of like a circus ring. There were a bunch of other dogs there, pulling their owners all over the place with their leashes. I noticed a giant Saint Bernard furiously digging a hole in the middle of the yard. "Stay away from that one," I whispered to Abby. "He looks like a bad influence."

Shep walked into the middle of the circle. "Okay, everyone, please listen up." All the humans turned around and paid attention. All the nonhumans did not.

"Tonight you begin a special journey with your dog," Shep continued. "A mythical journey of understanding. Of shared consciousness. Of mutual respect. Of—" He suddenly stopped. "Yo, what's that dog up to?"

Everyone turned and saw the giant Saint Bernard rolling around in the hole he had dug a few minutes before, which was deep enough to bury a small car in. Then the dog jumped up and started digging another hole right next to the first one.

"Sir?" Shep called to the dog's owner, a man wearing way too nice a suit to be hanging out in a dog shelter. "Can you please control your dog?"

The owner tried to smile but failed. "If I could control my dog, would I be here?"

I looked down at Abby. Suddenly, things didn't seem so bad. Abby might have been naughty, but at least she wasn't 120 pounds of naughty.

"Good girl," I told her. "You're being very well-behaved."

Abby took that moment to decide she was going to join the big bad Saint Bernard in the hole-digging party. She shot off like a spring, nearly separating my right arm from my body in the process.

"Abby!" I hollered, as I was going along for the involuntary ride. "Abby, stop!"

She didn't.

FACT: In a tug-of-war between a dog and an eleven-year-old boy, it's pretty easy to predict who's going to win.

In about twenty-eight seconds, Abby and the other dog made the shelter's yard look like the surface of the moon. Craters were everywhere.

The man in the suit looked at me. "There's nothing Thor likes more than digging holes," he said.

"Thor! Cool name."

The man nodded without smiling. "What's your dog called?"

"Abby," I said, slightly apologetically. For some reason, I thought Abby's name was a little lame.

"Cute little Abby," the man said, confirming my suspicions. "What's she in for?"

"My parents are tired of her destroying all my mom's expensive stuff," I said. "How about you?"

"This dog is the one thing in my life I can't control, and I want to change that." Then the man did smile, showing his super white teeth. "And I tend to get what I want."

Meanwhile, the two dogs had started exploring each other's . . . uh, well you know . . . anyway, it was a little awkward until Shep came over.

"Abby. Thor. Dudes. Give it a break." Shep had to be by far the most relaxed dog trainer in the whole world.

But Abby didn't stop. Instead she grabbed Thor's collar and started running around in circles. Thor, who weighed about three times as much as Abby, spun around slowly, looking down at the smaller dog. I think he was laughing inside.

"Seriously, Abby?" Shep asked, but Abby wasn't really in a listening mood at that point, because that's when she noticed the bin where the treats were, which I guess were used as rewards for dogs who actually obeyed orders.

Abby sprinted over to the bin and knocked it over. Biscuits and other assorted doggy delights went flying everywhere, which made the other dogs start howling, because they wanted in on the action. All of a sudden it sounded like an audition for *So You Think You Can Bark* (which is a TV show that doesn't exist, but it should).

Shep finally looked like he'd had enough. He walked over and scooped Abby up.

"Come with me, young lady," Shep said as he led Abby up onto a small stage in the front of the yard. "We're going to settle you down, and fast." Then he held his hand in the air. "Follow your star," he commanded.

Abby was squirming like she was stuck in quicksand.

"Settle," Shep whispered soothingly. "Now follow your

star." He looked out at the class. "This is an exercise that teaches both coordination and cooperation," he explained.

Everyone else stared at Shep as he slowly repeated the phrase over and over again, each time a bit slower, while raising his hand in the air. It seemed like he was hypnotizing Abby. "Follow your star . . . Follow your star . . . Fol . . . low . . . your . . . star . . ."

Finally, after about the twentieth time, Abby stopped wriggling around. Her head stayed high, with her eyes focused on Shep's hand as it went up in the air. Slowly Shep lowered his hand, but Abby's head stayed in the air, like she was actually following a star. She was completely still.

"Rest," Shep said, and Abby lowered her head.

"Wow," I said.

Thor's owner started clapping. "Very nice, very impressive," he said. "Can you do that with my dog?"

Shep looked up at the man. "I'm sorry, can you tell me your name again?"

"Swab," the man said. "Ned Swab."

Shep sighed. "Right. Well, Mr. Swab, as long as you just let me do my job, everything will be terrific. I'll get to all the dogs eventually."

PROFILE

Name: Ned Swab and his dog, Thor

Age: Over ten (Mr. Swab); Under ten (Thor)

Occupation: Whining (Mr. Swab); Digging (Thor)

Interests: Doing what they want (Both)

Mr. Swab looked mad. "We were here first," he snapped. "That's not exactly fair."

Shep quickly decided it wasn't worth arguing with the guy. "You got it, brother," he said. Then, under his breath, I heard him mutter, "There's one in every crowd."

The other trick Shep taught the dogs that first night was Drag and Drop, where each dog walks to a box that has one Frisbee and ten steak bones in it. The dogs are supposed to ignore the bones, grab the Frisbee, and drop it at Shep's feet. After each dog did it successfully, Shep rewarded them with Bury the Bone, where the dogs got to take one of the bones, chomp on it, then dig a hole in the yard and bury it. Of course, Thor and Abby loved that part.

All in all, it was pretty amazing how quickly Shep was able to get the dogs to do whatever he wanted. "Remember, dogs are like people—the more they do something, the happier and more comfortable they are with it," he said. "We don't want obedience to be a random event. When something happens often enough, it becomes more than a coincidence. It becomes a pattern."

Watching Abby go through her paces, I started looking forward to the great report I was going to give my parents. As the class was finishing up, though, I heard

Mr. Swab say "Bury the bone!" to Thor. Thor immediately started digging another giant hole.

"Sir, what are you doing?" Shep said. "I told the dogs to rest."

"I needed to make sure she knows who's the boss," Mr. Swab said. "That would be me, not you."

Shep shook his head but didn't say anything.

Abby immediately decided to join Thor in his digging. I shrugged apologetically at Shep, but he just smiled.

"It's not your fault, little man," he said. "But I'll tell you a secret: Sometimes the owners need more training than the dogs."

CHAPTER 8

"STOP TALKING WITH YOUR MOUTH FULL!" Irwin barked at lunch the next day.

"But I don't want the fish sticks to get cold," I explained.

Baxter reached over to my tray, grabbed a fish stick, and shoved it in his mouth. "There. Enough about the fish sticks."

FACT: Some people complain about cafeteria food, but that's just because they haven't discovered the completely delicious taste of fish sticks drenched in tartar sauce.

Irwin eyed Baxter nervously. "Jeez, take it easy." Baxter still had a few of his old bully habits, which scared Irwin a little. It was kind of like an old wart Baxter couldn't quite get rid of.

I got back to the business at hand. "So anyway, yeah,

like I was saying, Abby's going to obedience training. She chewed up one too many of my mom's shoes."

"You mean, like dog reform school?" Irwin asked.

I nodded grimly.

"Abby is great," Baxter said, "but she's not necessarily as super special as you think she is."

"Yes, she is," I said, in a tone that said *This is not up for discussion.*

So we stopped discussing it.

"Daisy is coming over to my house after school," Irwin announced.

"I thought we were going to the Boathouse," I said.

"I thought *you* said you had lacrosse practice," Irwin said. I suddenly got the feeling that Irwin was going to use my joining the lacrosse team as a way to spend time with Daisy *without* me.

"We can go to the Boathouse for, like, an hour before we have to go to practice," I told Irwin.

Baxter sighed. "Seriously, you two need to stop arguing over Daisy—it's so annoying." He looked for more food to steal from my tray, but my plate was empty.

"I need to go get some more chocolate milk," I said, getting up just as Chad Knight was walking by.

PROFILE

Name: Chad Knight

Age: Not sure, and I would never have the nerve to ask him

Occupation: Best athlete in the whole school

Interests: Being cool without even trying

We all froze.

Everybody froze for Chad Knight.

"Yo, Jimmy," Chad said.

"Yo, Chad," I tried to say normally, like I said "Yo, Chad" every day.

FACT: People like Chad Knight don't usually talk to people like me, unless absolutely necessary.

Baxter jumped up. "Hey, Chad. What's going on?"

"Not much," Chad said. Then he looked back at me. "Nice work in practice yesterday, Jimmy. Bring some of that to the game against Northport."

I blinked. "Um, okay."

Chad smacked my arm. "Cool. See you later."

Chad walked away, leaving Baxter standing there. He slowly sat back down, trying not to look embarrassed. Meanwhile, once the shock of seeing Chad talk to me started to wear off, Irwin slowly got his voice back.

"*Yo, Jimmy,*" he said, imitating Chad. "*Nice work in practice.*"

"Knock it off," I told Irwin.

Irwin laughed and shook his head. "Whatever.

That was weird. Does he think you're actually good at lacrosse?"

Baxter wasn't laughing, though. "Can we talk about something else?" he asked. I realized the idea of Chad praising my lacrosse skills didn't exactly make Baxter happy.

Irwin took a bite of his peanut butter sandwich (he always brought lunch from home, because his mom didn't trust cafeteria food) and took approximately two minutes to swallow it. Then he said, "The coolest kid in our grade just talked to Jimmy, and you want to talk about something else?"

"Yeah, I do," Baxter said. "Anything else."

But there wasn't much else to talk about, so we all ate silently until a voice said "Hey!" and we all looked up.

Daisy was coming over to sit with us, which we expected.

But she had someone else with her—Mara Lloyd. That was *un*expected.

"I thought Mara could sit with us today," Daisy explained.

"Uh . . ." said Irwin, which is exactly what I was thinking. Mara was one of Daisy's friends, but I'd never really talked to her before.

PROFILE

Name: Mara Lloyd

Age: The same as the rest of us, I think

Occupation: Daisy's non-CrimeBiters friend

Interests: Non-CrimeBiters stuff

"Hi, you guys!" Mara chirped. She was very chirpy. "What are you guys up to?"

"Uh . . ." I said, which was probably exactly what Irwin was thinking.

"Hey, Mara!" said Baxter. He had a lot of swagger, probably left over from his bully days. But like all bullies, the swagger only covered up the same insecurities the rest of us had. Which is why he then said, "Uh . . ."

"Are you guys talking CrimeBiters business?" Daisy asked. She turned to Mara. "Most lunches are spent talking about the CrimeBiters," she explained. "It's our gang and it's really fun. You could maybe join if you want."

Wait, what?!? My skin started to get hot with panic. I didn't even *know* Mara! Neither did the other guys! There's no way we could just let some random girl into our gang! It might change everything! It might ruin friendships! It might—

"Oh, ha-ha-ha-ha-ha!" Mara squeaked. She was also very squeaky.

FACT: Chirpy, squeaky girls make me nervous. As do non-chirpy, non-squeaky girls. Okay, fine, all girls make me nervous.

"That's okay!" Mara went on. "I'm not really interested in joining your silly club! Thanks anyway, though!"

Daisy laughed too. "No problem! It is kind of silly, but it's really fun." She turned to us. "Right, guys?"

Irwin, Baxter, and I just sat there, a little too stunned to say anything. The awkward silence lasted for about ten seconds. Or for about five years. Or maybe ten seconds that felt like five years.

"You know what?" Mara said finally. "I think maybe I'm going to go sit with Deirdre. She always gives me her extra potato chips."

And just like that, she was gone.

Daisy sat down.

"What was that about?" I asked her.

Daisy looked confused. "What was what about?"

"Mara saying our gang was silly," I said. "And you agreeing. That's what!"

"Oh, sorry. I didn't realize you'd be mad." Daisy started chomping on her sandwich. "But it is kind of silly, right? That's what makes it so fun!"

"I can't believe you would say that," Irwin said.

Daisy flashed her eyes at him. "What? You said pretty much the same thing the other day at the Boathouse!"

Baxter and I stared at Irwin, who looked like he'd just eaten a plate of boiled spiders.

"I didn't mean it," he said lamely.

I got up. "Well, this has been a delicious lunch," I announced. "Let's do it again really soon."

Daisy got up and put her hand on my shoulder. "I'm sorry, Jimmy. You know I love being in the CrimeBiters! I didn't mean anything bad. You can even have half my fish sticks!"

I looked at her, and suddenly all my bad feelings melted away.

FACT: It's hard to stay mad at girls. Especially ones named Daisy Flowers.

"It's okay," I said.

"But I think you owe me an apology too, for yelling," she added.

"Fine," I said. "I'm sorry."

And I sat down, and we finished our lunch. But somehow the food didn't taste as good.

Even the fish sticks.

CHAPTER 9

"THIS IS RIDICULOUS!" Misty moaned. It was a few days later, and my sister was doing what she always did at dinner, which was texting her friends when my parents weren't looking. "Why do I have to go?"

"It's your brother's first game," my mom said. "We're all going to support him."

My sister slumped her head down on her arm.

"Jarrod's going to be there," I said. I was referring to her boyfriend, who seemed like a nice enough guy, if you could forget that he has terrible taste in girls. "His brother is the best player on the team, and his dad is the coach."

"That's exactly what I'm worried about," said Misty, rolling her eyes. "Do you think I want to be there when Jarrod sees my little brother attempting to play lacrosse? That is like, *so* not going to happen."

"Hey," I said. "It just so happens that Coach Knight says I'm showing some real promise at goalie."

Misty let out a short, sharp laugh. "That's adorable!" Her shorts buzzed.

"No texting at the table," my mom said. "Give me the phone."

"Ugh!" Misty said, but she handed it over.

Then my dad's pocket started buzzing.

My mom stared at my dad. "Could be work—have to take it," he whispered apologetically. My dad didn't have a full-time job, but he was starting to get some projects here and there. Not that I have any idea what "projects" means.

As he got up, my sister said, "So why does he get to use his phone at dinner?"

"Do I really have to answer that?" said my mom.

Misty looked sheepish. "No."

"Does everyone see what I'm seeing?" I asked, changing the subject.

They looked at me. "No, what?"

I pointed at Abby, who was lying under my feet. "She hasn't begged for food once!" It was true. Abby was usually very persistent about requesting some of our dinner, but that night, she was being a very good little girl.

"Could the training be working already, after only two classes?" my mom asked. "That's impressive."

"I know, right?" I petted Abby proudly, and she thumped her tail in response.

"Oh, please," Misty said. "Do you want a medal just because she's starting to act like a normal dog?"

"Oh, please, yourself," I told her. "Abby is doing great. She hasn't made a peep this entire meal."

My mom smiled. "That's terrific!" I smiled back at her. It's true, Abby *was* doing great. In fact, she hadn't chewed up any of Mom's shoes in almost a week. But I didn't realize *how* great she was doing until later that night, when I got into bed. As usual, I opened the window so Abby could go on her nightly adventure. But she didn't make a move. She just perched on the windowsill, looking straight at me.

"Go on!" I said. "It's okay! You're not going to get in trouble, I promise."

But she just sat there, completely still.

Suddenly I got worried. "Is something wrong, Ab? Are you feeling okay? Did you eat some garlic by accident or something?"

Abby kept looking at me, and then she wagged her tail and gave me a lick. I felt relieved. She was fine! Then she turned back to the window and I was sure she was going to jump out. But instead, she slowly turned her head upward, and gazed up into the night sky.

I think she was following her star.

THE NEXT DAY I PLAYED in my very first lacrosse game, and it didn't take long before I understood why people who play sports walk around like they own the world.

We were the home team, playing against Northport, which is the next town over. When we took the field, a giant roar went up from our side of the field. "Go, Quietville!" "You can do it, Quietville!" "Beat Northport!" I looked up into the stands and couldn't believe it. It seemed like half the town was there, even though I knew it was probably more like seventy-five people. My parents were there, of course, clapping and yelling.

"Wow!" I said to Baxter. "Look at the size of our audience!"

"Audience?" he said. "Did you just say audience?" He shook his head in disgust.

FACT: If you're going to play sports, you need to learn the language.

"Fine, crowd! Whatever! It's just so awesome!" I smiled and waved at all the people, but then I realized that the players aren't supposed to pay attention to the people watching. That's the thing about being an athlete. Nothing else matters except the team. And winning, of course. And with the audience (I mean, crowd) on our side, we were going to win for sure!

And then the game started.

Northport was good. No, they were better than good. They were amazing. They had guys twice my size. They had guys twice the size of the biggest guy on our team, Chad Knight, who was twice my size. They were fast, and strong, and looked like they'd been playing together since some toddler lacrosse program. They zipped the ball around—*zip! zip! zip!*—until I got dizzy just watching them.

And then . . . they'd shoot.

LOOK OUT!

At first, I was petrified. The balls were coming so fast, my only hope was to not get killed. Before I had a chance to blink, they were winning, 6–2.

After the first quarter, Coach Knight gave the team a pep talk. "Guys! We haven't lost a game all season! I know they're good and we have a new goalie, but we can win this thing! Let's go!" Then he came over to check on me. "Everything okay, Jimmy?"

I nodded.

"Do you want to come out?"

My heart nodded YES, but my head shook NO.

"You got this," Coach said. "Just like in practice. You can do this!"

Then he patted me on the butt.

FACT: In sports, people pat other people on the butt all the time.

I went out for the second quarter, and just before the whistle, I snuck a look up into the crowd. My mom looked petrified; my dad looked completely stressed out. Only my sister looked normal. My annoying, obnoxious, pain-in-the-neck sister looked totally relaxed. Like she knew something nobody else knew. Then she noticed me looking at her, gave me a thumbs-up, and shouted "You can do this!"

And suddenly, my whole body went calm.

Soon enough, Northport was on the attack. They whipped the ball around, and then one of their biggest kids—he was twice the size of my *dad*—wound up and fired. But this time, I didn't duck. I didn't even flinch. I held my ground and followed the ball, and suddenly it seemed like everything was moving in slow motion. I put

my stick up and watched the ball float right into my netting.

"Great save, Jimmy!" hollered Coach Knight as the crowd roared. I quickly flicked the ball out to Chad, who weaved through the Northport defense and passed to an attacker on our team named Evan Wilson, who scored!

The whole place went nuts. Now we were only losing 6–3!

From that moment on, I started saving shots. I saved shots in the air, shots on the ground, shots on my left, and shots on my right. Of course, I couldn't quite save everything, which is why it was 8–6 at halftime.

Then, at the beginning of the third quarter, one of the kids on our team, Nick Hodges, was warming up behind our bench when he suddenly went down like a shot.

"OOOOOOWWWW!" he yelled, holding his right foot. A bunch of kids ran over to him, and we could immediately see that his ankle was blowing up like a balloon.

I bent down. "Are you okay?"

"I don't know!" he said, starting to cry. "I don't think so."

Coach Knight had reached us by then. "What's going on? What happened?"

Nick tried to talk through his tears. "I was just running along, and all of a sudden I tripped!"

Coach looked around and saw something on the ground near Nick. He bent down and pointed.

"Anyone know where the top to this storm drain is?!" he barked. "There's a big hole here!" We all shook our heads. "Well, Nick, it looks like you might have tripped over this darn thing."

"Everything okay?" asked the ref.

"Yup," said the coach. "Just a dumb accident. Another reason why we need to get a new field next year." Coach complained about the field all the time. He kept talking about how our archrivals LaxMax had the nicest field in the district. "How are we ever going to beat those guys if we have to play under these conditions?" he would mutter.

Coach helped Nick as he limped off the field. After another minute, we restarted the game, and we played even better, like we were doing it for Nick. But we still ended up losing by one, 13–12.

After the game, we found out that Nick's mom was worried that he had a sprained ankle, and they'd gone to the doctor. Everyone felt really bad for him, and sad that we lost, but we were still proud of our comeback. Even Coach said, "Way to fight." Then everyone in the stands came down onto the field, hugging us and consoling us. Irwin was there, looking like he was in shock.

"I didn't know you could play lacrosse like that," Irwin told me.

"Neither did I," I said. "Is Daisy here?"

Irwin shrugged. "I don't think so."

Before I had time to absorb that information, my parents and sister made their way over to me and gave me big hugs.

"Amazing!" they all shouted.

"Is that boy who got hurt going to be okay?" my mom asked.

"He hurt his ankle," I told them. "It totally stinks."

I saw Misty grinning, and I thought she was about to tell me how awesome I was, until I turned around and noticed that her boyfriend, Jarrod, was walking over.

"Hey, Jimmy, solid game," Jarrod said. "Looking like a real player out there."

"He's a great brother," Misty told him, which was pretty hilarious, since she'd never used the words *great* and *brother* in the same sentence before.

"Thanks," I said to them, before they started

whispering whatever it is that boyfriends and girl-friends whisper to each other.

I looked around. "Where's Abby?" I asked my parents.

"We decided to leave her home today," my dad explained. "We didn't want her to be a distraction. What if she tried to run out onto the field or something?"

I was disappointed that Abby wasn't there to see me play. Which makes me sound like a crazy person, I know.

My mom pointed. "Should we go over to say hi to Baxter?"

I looked over and saw him talking to his mom.

"Sure," I said.

We walked over to Baxter and Mrs. Bratford. When she saw us coming she gave a bright smile, but she didn't exactly look relaxed. Which made sense.

FACT: When you're talking to a person whose husband is in jail because of you, it can sometimes be an awkward conversation.

"Congratulations on a terrific game, young man," said Mrs. Bratford. "You are quite the lacrosse player."

"Thank you," I said.

Baxter looked a little awkward too. "I had no idea you would be so good," he said.

"That's what I said!" exclaimed Irwin.

"Well, I'm very impressed with both of you," said my mom.

Baxter shook his head. "I didn't play so good."

"So *well*," corrected Irwin.

We chatted for another minute or two until a whistle pierced the air. "Team meeting!" hollered Coach Knight. "Bring it in for a team meeting!"

All the parents and friends stood and watched as we gathered in a circle. "I'm very proud of you boys," the coach said. "You fought your tails off today and put a real scare into a very good team. Don't hang your heads—you gave it all you got. It's only one loss, we're still in the play-off hunt. We can still win the championship. And we're going to do it for our fallen teammate." Everybody clapped for Nick, even though he wasn't there. Then Coach held up a lacrosse ball. "Game ball today goes to our new goalie, Jimmy Bishop." He came over to me and shook my hand. "Pretty gutsy effort from a kid who just joined the team. You played a whale of a game today, son. A whale of a game."

As he handed me the ball, all the other kids cheered, and so did the crowd around us. I think it was the third-best feeling I ever had, after the day we adopted Abby and the first time Daisy came over to my house.

"Thanks, everyone," I said.

I was officially a lacrosse player.

CHAPTER 11

THE DAY AFTER THE NORTHPORT GAME, we were all on the roof of the Boathouse. Abby was with us, but she was hiding from the sun as usual, snoozing in the shade under the big elm tree.

"And then Jimmy got the game ball from the coach for being the player of the game," Irwin was telling Daisy. "Jimmy! Can you believe it?"

"Yes, I can," Daisy said, giving me a big smile. "I'm so happy for you, Jimmy."

"Thanks," I said. "It was a pretty awesome game. Too bad you had to miss it."

"I know, I'm so sorry!" Daisy said, slapping her head. "I was hanging out at Mara's and I totally lost track of the time. Are you really mad?"

"No," I said, telling the truth. I wasn't mad. I was more like semi-devastated.

Daisy looked concerned. "Well, you seem mad, so I

promise to make it up to you by going to all the rest of your games forever."

Irwin rolled his eyes at Daisy. "Why do you have to be so nice all the time? Doesn't it get tiring?"

"I'm not *being* nice, I *am* nice," Daisy said. "You should try it sometime."

"Oooooh, burn," said Baxter.

"What were you and Mara doing?" Irwin asked, trying to turn the tables on Daisy. "Was she telling you more about how silly the CrimeBiters are?"

"Of course not!" Daisy said, her eyes flashing. "We were just doing girl stuff. Something you wouldn't know anything about."

Irwin got quiet, the way he always did whenever Daisy got irritated with him.

I tried to change the subject. "Have you guys noticed anything different about Abby?"

They all looked at her, sleeping peacefully, then shook their heads.

"Nope," Baxter said. "Why?"

"I don't know," I said. "The obedience training is working and everything, but it kind of feels like she's changed a little."

"Isn't that the whole point?" Baxter asked.

Irwin snickered. "You mean she's not a vampire anymore?"

"Just forget it," I said.

"Can we stop arguing about everything?" Daisy said. "I don't get it. We're best friends! Let's go to my house—my mom is making caramel cupcakes."

"Baxter and I have practice," I said, dying a little inside.

Irwin frowned. "Seriously?"

"Yup," Baxter said. "Starts at four."

"That's annoying," Daisy said. She looked at Irwin. "I guess it will just be me and you again."

Irwin looked like his life had just changed forever—and for the better. "Uh, okay, yeah, we can totally do that."

"Hey, wait a second," I said, suddenly wishing I'd never seen a lacrosse stick.

"Let's go, Daisy," Irwin said gleefully. "See you guys later! Have a good practice!"

Baxter and I stood there for a few seconds, not saying anything. Irwin and Daisy leaving the Boathouse together was becoming a bad habit, like wearing the same shirt three days in a row.

"What's going on?" Baxter asked finally. "What are you so upset about?"

I watched Irwin and Daisy run off into the distance.

"I really love caramel cupcakes," I said.

CHAPTER 12

BY THE TIME I GOT TO PRACTICE I was still thinking about Irwin and Daisy having fun and cupcakes without me, which made me pretty mad, which might explain why I played unbelievably well. I saved everything in sight: Nothing got by me. Coach Knight said I was "in a zone," which apparently happens when you go to some alternate universe where you're the greatest athlete ever. It lasts for a while, and then you return to earth. But I was in a zone during the whole practice. At one point, Chad turned to me and said, "Jimmy, you're, like, the greatest goalie ever!" Baxter, who overheard, looked at me like he had no idea who I was.

After practice, I was waiting for my mom when I saw a car pull up and a familiar face get out.

Or should I say, a familiar wig.

I blinked to see if I was seeing things, but I wasn't. Mrs. Cragg was walking straight toward me.

PROFILE UPDATE

Name: Mrs. Cragg

Age: A lot

Occupation: My hunch is that she doesn't have one right now.

Interests: Trying to put the past behind her

In case you didn't know, Mrs. Cragg was Baxter's aunt, and my last babysitter. She was a little crazy, she hated Abby, and she helped her brother Barnaby steal my mom's valuable necklace.

Other than that, she was perfect.

She looked the same: her wrinkly face, her yellow teeth, and her bright red wig. But something was missing.

I think it was the scariness.

When she saw me, she stopped short. "Oh my, Jimmy! I certainly didn't expect to see you. Are you a lacrosse player?"

"I guess so, yeah. Uh, how are you, Mrs. Cragg?"

She seemed nervous. "Oh, I'm . . . doing much better, thank you. Back on my feet, as it were. I'm just picking up Baxter."

"He's still down on the field, getting his equipment together."

"I see." Mrs. Cragg smiled, and I suddenly felt sorry for her. Things must have been really hard for her since she and her brother got arrested. She didn't have to go to jail because she tried to help us in the end, but everyone in town knew who she was. Or, who she used to be.

"Well," she said. "Very nice to see you again, Jimmy. Take care."

"You too," I said, and I watched her walk down the hill.

"That was weird," I mumbled to myself.

"What was?" I heard a voice say. I turned around and Chad Knight was standing there.

"Nothing," I said. "Just waiting for my mom."

"Oh." Chad said. "Gotcha."

Then he said seven words I never thought I'd hear:

"Hey, Jimmy, what are you doing Saturday?"

I blinked. "Huh?"

"Are you around?" Chad asked. "Sometimes we have barbecues at my house after Saturday games, and it would be cool if you could come."

"Wow, uh, yeah, that'd be awesome," I said, even though I was immediately panicking a little in my head. Saturdays were usually reserved for the CrimeBiters.

"So you can come?" Chad asked.

"Yeah, totally. Thanks."

Baxter, meanwhile, was walking up the hill with his aunt. When he saw me talking with Chad, he immediately came over. "Oh, hey, uh, have you guys seen my, uh, my baloney sandwich?"

FACT: When coming up with an excuse to join a conversation, you need to do better than "Have you guys seen my baloney sandwich?"

"Nope," I said.

"Oh, okay. I thought I dropped it around here." He lingered, pretending to look for his nonexistent sandwich. "So, what are you guys talking about?"

"Jimmy's gonna come over to my house after the game on Saturday to hang out," Chad said, apparently completely unaware that what he was saying would crush Baxter's soul. "Toss the ball around, maybe swim a little bit, that kind of thing."

"Oh, cool," Baxter said to Chad, but he was staring at me.

"Yeah, uh, probably just for a little while," I said. Chad looked confused, so I added, "I usually have this thing I do with my friends every Saturday."

"What kind of thing?" Chad asked.

Baxter was looking at me, waiting for me to answer. I could have so easily said *we have this gang, and it's called CrimeBiters, and it's really cool, and you can be in it if you want, and it's made us all really brave, and our job is to* protect Quietville from crime, with the help of my dog, Abby, and it's the best and most fun thing in my life, and I love doing it with my best friends—but I didn't.

Instead, I just said, "Oh, nothing. It's cool. I can probably skip it."

Right at that moment, I felt about as brave as a mouse.

CHAPTER 13

"I GOT A JOB!" my dad announced that night at dinner.

Misty and I looked up but didn't stop eating. Mom wasn't home yet, as usual, and it was Wednesday night, which meant we always ordered the best fried chicken in the world, from Beak-a-boo. An announcement like this, no matter how important, wasn't going to distract us from our dining duty.

Misty chomped on a wing. "For real?" Dad hadn't had a full-time job for the last few years. It wasn't something we talked about very much.

"Well, that's a good question," Dad said. "It could become real, if I play my cards right."

"Congratulations, Dad," I said, taking a big gulp of lemonade.

"Thanks," he said. "The thing is, though, it might mean we need to find some after-school help."

"Dad!" snapped Misty. "I've told you a thousand times, I don't need a babysitter."

"Fine," my dad said. "Let's call it a chauffeur, then. Whatever you want to call this person, we're going to need an adult around here Tuesdays and Thursdays, starting next week."

"How about Mrs. Cragg?" I blurted out, before even realizing that idea had formed in my brain.

My father and sister stared at me like I had two heads. If I could have, I would have stared at myself like I had two heads too.

"What the heck are you talking about?" said my dad.

"I don't know," I said. "I just thought . . . maybe she's not so bad."

"Not so bad?" said my sister. "NOT SO BAD? She's a criminal! She's a thief! She almost killed you!" That last one was a slight exaggeration, but still—my sister had a point.

"I saw her today after practice," I told them. "She was picking up Baxter and she seemed different. Like, sad and lonely." I wiped my mouth with my shirt. "And I don't really blame her for what happened. I mean, I do, but I don't. She was so scared of her brother. She did whatever he told her to do, because she was worried that he would hurt her. But eventually she turned against him. She even tried to help us." It was true. She helped us escape and tried to protect us from her brother in the end.

"What about when she locked Abby in the closet?" asked my dad. "I can't believe you would ever forgive her for that."

"I know," I said. "But at the same time, Abby had stolen her dinner and vomited all over her hair."

"Wig," corrected Misty.

"Right. Wig." I took a bite of a drumstick. "Anyway, I think maybe sometimes people deserve a second chance."

My dad sat back in his chair and sighed. "Okay, let's think about this for a minute," he said. "I have to say, this is the last thing I would have thought of, given everything that happened. But I'm really impressed with your attitude here, Jimmy, and I'm willing to consider it. If Mom is okay with the whole idea, then we can give it a try."

"Great," I said. Helping Mrs. Cragg made me feel good, for some reason.

"So I guess she's not in jail, huh?" my dad asked.

I shook my head. "Nope. Community service."

"You're BOTH nuts," Misty said. "And by the way, Abby HATED Mrs. Cragg. This is NOT going to go well at ALL."

FACT: Sisters TALK like THIS a lot, where they REALLY EMPHASIZE certain WORDS.

My dad looked at me. "Yeah, that's a good point. What *about* Abby?"

"No problem," I said, but I suddenly started panicking inside. I hadn't thought about that. I looked down at Abby, who was hanging out under the kitchen table, playing with one of my old sneakers I didn't wear anymore. "We have obedience training tonight," I said. "I'll talk to Shep about it. He'll know what to do."

"You can start by making sure Abby doesn't rip Mrs. Cragg's wig off her head," Misty said.

After my mom got home, my dad mentioned the Mrs. Cragg idea to her, and the first thing she said was, "Just don't let her near the kitchen." That was a reference to

Mrs. Cragg's habit of cooking the most disgusting food ever known to humankind.

"Will do," said my dad and I, at the same time.

"Are you sure this is what you want?" my mom asked me.

I nodded. "I'm sure."

"Okay," said my mom. "Let's try it."

Later that night, when my mom was driving Abby and me to obedience training, I turned the radio on and she turned it right back off. That was a sign she wanted to talk.

Oh, well.

"Are you okay with Dad getting a job?" she asked.

"Are you?" I asked back.

She nodded. "Of course! The only thing we all want is for Dad to be happy. This might be important to help make that happen."

"Are you saying Dad isn't happy staying home and taking care of us?" I knew the question wasn't really fair, but I asked it anyway.

"Of course he is," she said. "But that's a different kind of happy. It's 'being a dad' kind of happy. But some people need more than that. Some people need 'I love my job' kind of happy too."

"Like you, you mean?" I guess I was in an unfair-question kind of mood.

My mom turned the radio on. I guess she didn't really want to talk after all.

"I love this song," she said, even though a commercial was playing.

CHAPTER 14

"WASSUP, PRINCESS?" Shep said to Abby when we walked into class. He scratched her under her chin, right where she loved it. "You ready to be good?"

"Oh, she's ready," I said.

Shep nodded. "Let's do this." He clapped his hands together, and all the dogs and owners gathered in a circle, the way we always did.

"Tonight," Shep announced, "you are going to trust your dogs."

We all looked at each other.

"Meaning, you are going to let them learn on their own," he explained. "When you release their leashes, you release their ability to grow."

Nobody moved.

"Release the leashes," Shep repeated.

As one, we all dropped the leashes. Most of the dogs

stayed calm and well-behaved, but Thor started jumping around and spinning in circles. Thor hadn't really improved his behavior much at all since the classes began, and it totally drove Mr. Swab crazy. It was pretty enjoyable to watch, to be honest with you.

"Thor!" Mr. Swab hollered. "Up on your feet!" But instead Thor rolled over and scratched his back on the wood floor. Mr. Swab looked like he was about to have a stroke. "This class isn't working at all!"

Shep rolled his eyes. "With some dogs it takes a bit longer." He pointed at Abby. "Now this girl here, she seems to be at the head of the class."

Abby looked up at him and wagged her tail.

"I think your dog's hilarious," I told Mr. Swab. "He's got a great personality." I looked at Abby, who was sitting perfectly still, waiting to be told what to do next. *You could use a little bit of that personality*, I thought, then immediately felt guilty for thinking it.

Mr. Swab, meanwhile, kept staring at his dog and scowling. "Is there a money-back guarantee for this class?"

Shep ignored him. "Today we're going to try something different," he said. "I'm going to encourage the dogs to behave badly—should be perfect for Thor—and you're going to have to overrule me. They need to start listening to you more than me. I call this exercise Just Chew It."

We headed outside and there were a bunch of old chairs lined up in the yard. One leg on each chair was wrapped in bacon. The dogs immediately got hyper. Thor started howling like a hyena.

"Oh, for crying out loud," said Mr. Swab.

Shep pointed at the chairs. "Go!" he commanded, and each dog ran to a chair and started gnawing on the bacon. It was a madhouse of grabbing, licking, and slurping.

FACT: There are very few things that dogs like more than bacon. Actually, now that I think about it, there are no things a dog likes more than bacon.

"Now tell your dogs to stop!" Shep urged. "Tell them to rest!"

I walked over to Abby. "Stop!" I hollered. "Abby, rest! Rest now!"

Amazingly enough, she stopped.

Meanwhile, I looked over and saw that Thor was so desperate to get at his bacon that he ripped the leg right off his chair. "Stop!" Mr. Swab yelled, but Thor looked like he couldn't care less—he just kept on doing his thing.

Believe it or not, I felt a little jealous of Mr. Swab right about then.

Shep came over to me. "Abby is really doing fantastic," he said.

"I know," I said. "It's crazy. She used to be completely out of control."

"You don't seem all that thrilled about her progress."

"No, I am!" I insisted. "She was driving my parents nuts. Well, my mom, really. So I'm happy and relieved that she's doing so great."

Meanwhile, Mr. Swab had put Thor back on his leash. "That was a stupid exercise," he was saying, to anyone who would listen. "How am I supposed to get my dog to just stop eating bacon?"

Shep looked at him. "You're used to things going your way, aren't you?" he asked.

Mr. Swab looked back. "If you're asking if I'm competitive and like to win, well then yes, I am and I do. It's a dog-eat-dog world out there, pal. It's how I got to where I am today."

Shep smiled. "By the looks of things, it's more of a dog-eat-bacon world," he said.

CHAPTER 15

THE NEXT DAY AT LUNCH, I really wanted to tell the other guys about the obedience training. Baxter was the only one there so far, so he was my first victim.

"And Abby was acting perfectly, and this other dog Thor was acting like a lunatic, and I was wishing that it was the other way around! Isn't that crazy?"

Baxter nodded the way someone nods when they don't really care one way or the other.

"Well, you had to be there," I said. "It was really weird."

"Okay." Baxter looked way more interested in his meatball hero.

Suddenly we heard footsteps behind us. I heard Daisy's voice say, "Let's ask these guys!"

Baxter and I turned around to see Daisy and Mara, getting ready to sit down at our table.

Oh great, I thought. *Here we go again.*

"Ask us what?" I said.

Daisy was holding a sheet of paper in her hand. "Look what Mara found in her locker!"

Daisy handed me the sheet, which had been ripped out of a notebook. It had four words written on it, in giant red marker:

I REALLY LIKE YOU.

"What is it?" Baxter asked, leaning over my shoulder.

"Mara has a secret admirer," Daisy explained.

I was confused. "A what?"

"She's been finding these notes hidden inside her desk for, like, a week. One said YOUR HAIR IS PRETTY. Then the next one said NICE DRESS." Daisy took the paper back from me. "And now this one."

Mara nodded in excitement. "That's right! I can't figure out who it is and so I thought I'd ask Daisy if the CrimeBiters could help me!"

Irwin walked up to the table with a tuna-fish-and-onion sandwich. (In case you're wondering, yup, it smelled as bad as it sounds.) "What are you guys doing?"

"We have a new crime to solve," Baxter said. "The case of the boy who likes Mara's hair."

"That's not a crime," I said. "That's a mystery. We're

not the MysteryBiters. We're the CrimeBiters. And besides, I thought you thought our gang was silly. Now you want our help?"

Mara looked at me like I'd just thrown something at her.

"You're not being very nice," Daisy told me.

"Sor-RY," I answered.

"Let me see that," Irwin said. He grabbed the note out of Daisy's hand and started studying it as if he were examining the just-discovered first draft of the Declaration of Independence. In other words, very, very carefully.

"While technically this may not be a crime," Irwin said finally, "it is still a case that needs to be solved, and I am willing to help solve it." He eyed me coldly. "Even if you and Baxter are too busy with lacrosse to participate."

"Yay!" Mara exclaimed.

"Oooh, goodie!" Daisy said. "Mysteries are kind of fun and romantic."

"I don't think it's fun and romantic at all," I said. "You guys go solve your little mystery. Let us know what happens." I nudged Baxter's elbow and rolled my eyes. "We're dying to know, aren't we, Baxter?"

"Actually, I'd like to help," Baxter said. "I can meet you guys after practice."

"Fine!" I said, picking up my tray. "I'm going to go eat lunch somewhere else."

"Jimmy, come on," Daisy said, but I was already walking away. I spotted Chad and some of the other lacrosse kids and headed over to their table.

"Hey, Jimmy!" Chad said. "Take a seat."

"Cool, thanks," I said, sitting down.

"What took you so long?" said Billy Clay, one of Chad's friends. I didn't really know Billy, since he didn't play lacrosse, but I'd heard rumors he was an amazing basketball player. "I was beginning to think you were going to sit with those dorks forever."

I felt my ears start to turn red, but I didn't say anything. Luckily, Chad did.

"Mind your own business," he told Billy. Then he turned to me. "Don't worry about him—he can be a real jerk."

I was still busy trying to decide if *I* was being a jerk when the bell rang.

End of lunch.

CHAPTER 16

THE MINUTE I WALKED IN THE DOOR AFTER SCHOOL, I recognized the whistling.

"Hello?" I called.

"In here," came the voice that used to make my skin prickle with dread.

I went into the kitchen and there she was: Mrs. Cragg, my onetime nemesis, the woman who made me eat fried green blech for dinner, the woman who tried to steal my mom's favorite necklace.

And here's the crazy part: I was happy to see her.

And here's the other crazy part: Something smelled *delicious*.

"Jimmy!" she said. "It's wonderful to see you."

"Hi, Mrs. Cragg. I didn't realize you were going to be here today."

She laughed. "Well, your dad asked me to come by this afternoon because he had to take his car in for servicing." She wiped her hands on a towel. "He told me you're the one whose idea it was to give me another chance. I want you to know how much that means to me, Jimmy. You're a very good boy."

"Well, you were nice to us at the end and helped us." I looked at the stove. "Are you cooking something? No offense or anything, but my mom said you weren't allowed in the kitchen."

She laughed. "None taken! Yup, I'm cooking something up, but it's not for you."

"It's not?"

"Nope."

She looked down, and I followed her gaze to the floor, where there was a dog happily wagging her tail, looking up adoringly at Mrs. Cragg.

You want to know who that dog was?

Abby.

Yup.

ABBY!

My mind went blank with shock.

FACT: Sometimes it takes about ten seconds for your brain to believe what your eyes are seeing.

All I could say was one word.

"Huh?"

"I know," Mrs. Cragg said, "isn't it wonderful? We've become the best of friends." She clapped her hands together and whistled cheerfully as she bent down to pet Abby, who licked Mrs. Cragg's hand in return. Then Mrs. Cragg gave her a small piece of the sausage she was cooking.

FACT: Sausage will make a dog love you really fast.

Holy smokes, I thought to myself. Mrs. Cragg had turned into a combination of Mrs. Doubtfire and Dr. Dolittle.

"Your dad said to tell you that he'll be home around suppertime," Mrs. Cragg said. "Do you have any particular plans this afternoon? Will you be watching that TV show you like, or reading those vampire books you always read?"

"Actually, no," I said. "I don't really do that stuff that much anymore."

"Oh? And why is that?"

"I've gotten real busy lately. I have a group of friends now and I'm on the lacrosse team and I have to take Abby to obedience training and stuff like that."

"Well, I think that's terrific," said Mrs. Cragg. "You don't want to be spending too much time by yourself. It's good to be out and about."

"I agree." I sat down at the kitchen table and called to Abby, who jumped up onto my lap. "How did you and Abby become such good friends so quickly?" I didn't say the part about how the last time they saw each other was when Mrs. Cragg's brother tried to kidnap Abby.

"Well, treats help, of course," Mrs. Cragg said. "And it turns out she doesn't hold a grudge. She's decided to give me a second chance. And frankly, I must say, she seems much better behaved."

"Yeah, I know," I said. "She's in obedience training, and she's one of the best in the class."

"How wonderful!"

"I know, it's great, I'm really proud of her," I said, which was half-true. I was really proud of her. I just wasn't sure how great it was.

Mrs. Cragg reached into a closet and pulled out a large, gift-wrapped box. "Speaking of second chances . . . I'm very grateful, Jimmy. And to thank you, I've brought you and your little pal a little present."

"Wow!" I said, looking at the box. "You didn't have to do that."

"I wanted to." She smiled. "Go ahead."

I tore off the wrapping paper, and there was a long wooden box with a bone design all over it, and a really comfy-looking pillow inside. ABBY was spelled out in handwriting on the side of the box.

"Wow!" I exclaimed. "It says Abby! This is totally awesome." I looked at it again. "What is it?"

Mrs. Cragg smiled, and I noticed that she'd gotten her yellow teeth whitened since the last time I'd seen her. (Or maybe she just got a new set of teeth.) "I figured, if I'm going to get you to like me, the first thing I need to do is get your dog to like me," she said. "I remember how she likes to sleep in your closet during the day, so I thought I'd give her a little bed to sleep in."

I looked at her. I immediately recognized exactly what this box looked like—a coffin! Which, of course, is what vampires sleep in.

FACT: A coffin-shaped bed is a gift you should only give under very special circumstances.

Did I ever tell Mrs. Cragg that I thought Abby was a vampire? I couldn't remember.

"This is amazing, Mrs. Cragg. Thank you so much." Then I bent down. "Abby, look! A new bed! Do you want to try it out?"

Abby went over to the bed and sniffed it but didn't get in.

"Maybe later," Mrs. Cragg said.

I wasn't about to give up. "Abby, are you sure? This is perfect for you! And you love napping during the day!"

Abby licked my hand and walked away.

I shook my head. "I don't know," I told Mrs. Cragg. "It's

like . . . she's so much better behaved now, but she's changed so much that sometimes I don't even recognize her. All the stuff she used to love . . ." But my voice trailed off before I finished the sentence.

"Sometimes change is a good thing," Mrs. Cragg told me gently. "Just look at me."

I smiled. "Yeah, that's true. It's nice to see you so . . . nice."

Mrs. Cragg laughed. "Miracles do happen, right? So give her a chance. She might change, but she'll always be your Abby."

"I guess so," I said.

We sat quietly for a minute, then she asked, "Do you have some after-school plans?"

I nodded. "We're all meeting at Irwin's house. Usually we go to the Boathouse, but his mom is finally picking up our club sweatshirts today."

"How fun!" said Mrs. Cragg.

But as she poured me a bowl of cereal (Sugar Flakies, my favorite), I noticed Mrs. Cragg's face turn a little sad. "I remember the Boathouse," she said. I realized she was thinking about the last time she was there—when the police finally caught her brother, Barnaby Bratford, after we trapped him.

"I'm sorry I brought it up," I said.

She smiled at me. "You have nothing to apologize for."

After eating, I hopped up. "I should go. I think they're waiting for me. Thanks again for the cool bed for Abby."

"Of course!" Mrs. Cragg walked me to the front door. "Have a wonderful time."

I looked at her standing there, with Abby nuzzled up against her leg.

I guess it's true what they say.

Anything *is* possible.

CHAPTER 17

WHEN I WALKED INTO IRWIN'S KITCHEN, Irwin, Daisy, and Baxter were already wearing their sweatshirts, chattering excitedly—but when they saw me coming, they immediately got quiet.

"Those look great!" I said.

"Yours is in the living room," Irwin said.

"Cool." I ran into the other room, put the sweatshirt on, ran to the bathroom to see what it looked like, and ran back into the kitchen, all in about five seconds. I waited for everyone to tell me how awesome I looked. But they didn't say a thing.

A minute went by.

"What were you guys just talking about?" I finally asked.

"Nothing, really," Baxter said. "You're a little late, though."

Daisy crinkled her nose at me. "Nice of you to show up, Mr. Lacrosse Star."

"Star? Ha!" I said. "I've only played one game so far."

Irwin's eyes narrowed. "You did sit with Chad at lunch today."

"And aren't you going to his house after the game on Saturday?" asked Daisy.

"Yeah," added Baxter, "aren't you?"

I immediately realized what was happening. Chad was one of those kids that we always used to make fun of,

because we knew we could never be anything like him. And now my friends were starting to wonder if I was becoming *exactly* like him.

"Yeah, so he invited me to a barbecue one time, so what," I said. "What did you guys want me to do, say no?"

The three of them looked at one another, but nobody said anything.

"Hey, guess who my new babysitter is?" I said finally, changing the subject.

"We give up," said Baxter.

"I'll give you a hint: She wears a red wig."

Irwin nearly fell off his chair. "You gotta be kidding me."

"Nope. Not kidding."

"Wow," said Baxter. "My aunt? Really?"

"Was this your parents' idea?" asked Daisy.

"Actually, it was my idea," I said. "I know it sounds crazy, but when I saw her picking up Baxter the other day, she looked really sad. I thought she deserved another chance."

Daisy smiled. "That's really awesome, Jimmy," she said, which made me feel a warm glow all over.

"Wow," said Baxter. "I bet she really appreciated it."

"She did." I was feeling better. Like the guys liked me again.

"I think it's a little weird, actually," Irwin said. "How do you know that she's really changed? That she's not going to do the same crazy stuff again?" Irwin looked at Baxter. "No offense or anything, but your aunt pretty much scared the bejeepers out of me."

"It's okay," said Baxter.

"Well, I think it's great," Daisy said to me. "I think you did a nice thing."

"Me too," Baxter added.

"Thanks," I said.

We all looked at Irwin, to see if he was going to continue being irritated by everything I said or did.

"We made some progress on the secret admirer case," he said finally. "It turns out that all the notes came from a Scooby-Doo notebook."

Daisy nodded. "So we're going to meet by the buses after school tomorrow and see who has a Scooby-Doo notebook or Scooby-Doo backpack."

"Jimmy and I can't," Baxter said. "We have lacrosse."

"That's right," I said. "Let's just do it next week."

"I'd rather do it tomorrow," Irwin said.

"What's the rush?" I asked. "It's not like someone is stealing jewelry all over town or anything."

As soon as I said it, I looked at Baxter, whose face turned red.

"Sorry," I said.

"It's okay," he said, for the second time in five minutes. Jeez, it must have been hard to be him sometimes.

"You guys don't have to come if you don't want," Irwin said. "But Daisy and I have made up our minds. We've been waiting for four months for a new case, because we live in the most un-crime-y place on earth. So now that we have an actual mystery, we want to solve it. Right, Daisy?"

Irwin looked at Daisy with a pleading expression on his face. She glanced back and forth from Irwin to me. It was obvious she was torn over what to do. She knew I was mad when they went and had cupcakes without me after our last meeting. She wouldn't hurt my feelings again, right?

Finally, she nodded. "Sorry, Jimmy, but I agree with Irwin. He and I will meet tomorrow and report back."

Wrong.

CHAPTER 18

FACT: If someone made a list called TEN THINGS THAT WILL NEVER HAPPEN TO JIMMY BISHOP, "Being cheered on by cheerleaders" would probably be at the top.

YET, THERE THEY WERE.

We had cheerleaders!

They weren't at the last game because they only cheered at weekend games, but there they were—ten girls with skirts and pom-poms, jumping up and down and shouting our names as if we were their favorite people in the world.

I was thrilled, but my mom wasn't. "I find cheerleading a hopelessly old-fashioned tradition," she said as we saw them practicing. "Why is it that the girls are always cheering for the boys? Why aren't the boys cheering for the girls?"

My dad snorted. "Because that would just be wrong, that's why."

"You're a pig," my mom told him.

"That's a little harsh," he told her back.

"Is not."

"Is too."

"What is this, first grade?" complained Misty. She was there completely and totally against her will, by the way. I knew that because before we left the house, she told me, "I'm going to this game completely and totally against my will."

"Hi, Jimmy!" squealed a few of the cheerleaders as I got out of the car. "Good luck today!"

"Thanks!" I told them. "I'm going to do my best!"

My sister looked like she was about to throw up.

I ran out to join my teammates, and we began stretching. The team we were playing, Glenvale, pulled up in their bus and started warming up on the other half of the field. Coach Knight pulled me aside and pointed at a huge kid wearing number 27.

"He's the one you have to watch," Coach said. "He's got a wicked lefty shot."

"Got it, Coach."

"Go get 'em out there!" And he smacked me on the top of my helmet, which stung a little bit, not that I was going to say anything about it.

Just before the game began, I looked up into the crowd.

"I already checked to see if Daisy and Irwin came after all," Baxter said. "They didn't."

"Whatever." I picked up my stick. "We've got a game to win."

The game was close. That big lefty was a great player, and he scored against me in the first and second quarters. But no one else did, and at halftime, the score was tied, 2–2.

We all huddled up on the sideline to get something to drink and listen to the coach give us our pep talk. "So far, so good!" urged Coach Knight. "I like how hard you guys are working out there! But the one thing I need you to do is—"

CRACK!!!

Coach was interrupted by the loud, unmistakable sound of wood cracking. We all looked around and realized the only wood anywhere around us was the bench we were all sitting on.

Then we heard it again . . . three short, sharp sounds.

CRACK . . . CRACK . . . CRACK!!!

And in an instant, the left side of the bench completely collapsed, and three kids—Marty Linsky, Jeff Provost, and Cedric Feathers—crashed to the ground in a heap.

"OWWW!" they all hollered.

The rest of us all jumped up like we'd been shot out of a cannon, while a bunch of adults ran down to the field to find out what had happened. Marty had a cut on his shin, Jeff was holding his knee, and Cedric was lying on his stomach, saying his butt was killing him.

Coach Knight started running around, hollering at anyone who would listen. "That was crazy! We were having our halftime meeting and the bench just buckled! The whole thing folded like a cheap tent!"

"First an exposed storm drain on the field, and now this!" said one parent.

"We need to find a new place to play, once and for all!" said another.

"Too bad our kids don't play for LaxMax," said a third. "This would never happen at their field."

"What's the deal with LaxMax?" I asked Chad. "People talk about them like they're gods or something. Are they really so great?"

"Their benches don't break, I know that much," he said.

While the parents took care of the kids, the ref came over and asked Coach if we wanted to play the second half. Coach looked at the hurt players, and they all nodded. After a minute, Coach Knight nodded too.

"Yes sir," he told the ref. "We've got a game to win."

Everyone cheered, including the kids who got hurt, and we took the field.

The second half was just as close as the first. Our team was really fired up after the halftime excitement, and we scored two quick goals in the third quarter, but their lefty kid scored one and then somebody else on their team scored a lucky goal when his shot deflected off Baxter and past me, into the net.

"Baxter!" I hollered.

"What?" he hollered back. "It's not my fault! I was trying to block the shot!"

"Well, you blocked it right into our goal!"

He stared at me and shook his head. "Buzz off," he mumbled, but I could tell he felt lousy, which suddenly made me feel lousy.

It was 4–4 with three minutes left in the game when

Chad took the ball up the field, faked out about three guys, then passed to Eric Pacilio, who snuck an under-handed shot past their goalie. We were ahead! Their team called time-out.

There was no bench to sit on, so we all gathered around the coach, ready for our final instructions.

"I'm going to make some changes, just for the last few minutes," he said. "Baxter, take a little break."

Baxter looked shocked. "You want me to come out?"

Coach Knight patted him on the back. "You're doing great, son, but you seem a little tired. I'm going to put Gendels back there on defense just to close things out."

Baxter slowly took his helmet off and went to sit down on the bench. I couldn't help but think that maybe it was because I'd blamed him for their last goal.

I went and sat next to him for a second. "Hey, Baxter. I'm really sorry."

But he just looked at me and didn't say anything.

"Let's go get 'em!" hollered the coach. I didn't have time to think about hurting Baxter's feelings, or Daisy or Irwin skipping the game to search for Mara's secret admirer, or anything else other than protecting our lead. That's what athletes have to do—block everything out and concentrate. It's kind of like what Hank Barlow has to do when he's trying to solve a crime, or Jonah Forrester when he's on the trail of a bad guy.

Hank and Jonah! Boy, I hadn't thought about them for a while. They were like two old friends that I hadn't seen a lot of lately—

"Bishop! Why are you still sitting there? GET GOING!"

Uh-oh. The coach was in my face, hollering, because I was still sitting on the bench next to Baxter, and the game was about to start again. I was thinking about focusing so much that I totally forgot to focus! Baxter was watching me, sipping a cup of water.

"Get out there and hold 'em," he said.

I nodded at him gratefully. "Thanks. I'll try."

I ran out onto the field. We were still winning by one goal, there were two minutes left to play, and we had the ball. Everything looked like it was under control. But all of a sudden, with twenty seconds to go, the left-handed kid stole the ball and started storming down the field right toward me.

"Guard him!" I screamed at my teammates. "Guard him!" But he sprinted past them like they weren't even there.

Three seconds later, the big lefty was bearing down on me like a freight train that was out of control. Or more accurately, a freight train that was in *total* control.

I gripped my stick tighter and bounced on my toes, the way Coach Knight taught me.

Finally, when he was about fifteen feet away from me, he pulled his stick back into a shooting position. "Argghh!" he yelled, and fired.

Or so I thought.

I was surprised that he was shooting from so far away, but I reacted anyway. I went to where the shot was heading, thinking, *I got this*. The only problem was, there was no ball. It was a fake! I was already sprawled on the ground, trying to save an imaginary shot, when the kid pulled his stick back and fired *again*, this time for real.

"You're toast!" I heard him say, laughing.

Everything felt like slow motion as I watched the ball go through the air. In under a second I thought about how hard it would be to face my team after being faked out of my shoes on the last play of the game. I thought about how glad I was that Daisy and Irwin weren't there to see me get embarrassed like that. And I thought that maybe this was a sign that I should go back home, play with Abby, and watch *STOP! POLICE!* on TV, just like the good old, uncomplicated pre-lacrosse days.

I swear, I thought all that in under a second.

FACT: It's amazing what the brain can do when it puts its mind to something.

QUESTION: Does a brain even have a mind?

The last thing I thought was, *No. I can't let this happen.*

And somehow, just as the ball was about to cross the line, I dove back across the goal mouth, flung my stick across my body, and knocked the ball away.

SAVE!

"Are you kidding me?!?" shouted the kid, shocked.

The buzzer went off, the game ended, and the whole place went nuts. We'd won! Before I even realized what was happening, half the team was running over to me, lifting me up onto their shoulders, and carrying me off the field. The other half of the team was in a circle in the middle of the field, jumping on top of each other. Even the three kids who'd been hurt by the crashing bench were limping around, high-fiving and celebrating with everyone else. "Easy, guys! It's just one game!" Coach Knight kept yelling, but no one was listening to him.

Even Baxter smacked me on the back. "Great job, Jimmy," he said, and it really seemed like he meant it.

When I got off the field, I jumped into my parents' arms, and we hugged and screamed for joy. Misty picked her head up out of her phone long enough to give me a quick hug and admit, "That was pretty amazing." Her boyfriend, Jarrod, smacked me on the shoulder and said, "Dude!" Soon enough a ton of other people came over, and it seemed like I was getting congratulated by half the town.

In the middle of the happy craziness, I felt a tap on my shoulder. Irwin and Daisy were standing there with Mara Lloyd, and they all had huge smiles on their faces.

I couldn't believe it—they'd made it after all!

"You guys came!" I exclaimed. "That's awesome! Wasn't that ending the craziest thing you ever saw?"

As we all stood there, with people cheering all around us, it seemed like everything was finally working out the way it was supposed to. A fairy-tale ending!

Then real life got in the way.

CHAPTER 19

AS SOON AS IRWIN AND DAISY LOOKED at each other, I knew that I'd been wrong. They hadn't been at the game at all.

"We cracked the case," Daisy announced.

"What do you mean, you cracked the case?" I asked. "What case?"

I was standing there, dripping with sweat in my lacrosse uniform, the celebration of our big win happening all around me, people slapping me on the back and calling me a hero, but all I wanted to know was what Daisy was talking about.

"The secret admirer case," Irwin said.

Now I was starting to get annoyed. They interrupted the greatest moment of my sports life—a life which, I admit, was only about a week old—for a silly fake case about some kid sending some girl goofy notes?

Baxter came over. "What's going on?"

"They cracked the all-important case," I said.

"Well, we didn't quite crack it," Daisy said. "But we have some good leads. Yesterday after school we spotted four kids with Scooby-Doo notebooks, and asked them each to write down their three favorite colors on a piece of paper. We told them it was a project for school. Now we're heading to the clubhouse to compare handwriting samples."

"This is so amazing!" Mara said to me excitedly. "I can't believe I made fun of you guys. Being a CrimeBiter must be so cool!"

"Maybe one day you can join the gang," Irwin said. Mara giggled.

"Are you guys serious?!" I said, losing patience. "I already told you, this isn't a case! It's just some kid who is too shy to tell a girl he likes her." I looked at Irwin. "You should know something about that."

Irwin gave me a wounded look. "We're all going to the clubhouse to examine the evidence, Jimmy, with or without you."

"Come on," Daisy said. "You're coming, right?"

"I can't."

They all stared at me.

"What do you mean?" Irwin said.

"I mean, I couldn't go even if I wanted to." I pointed to Chad Knight, who was standing with Eric and Stefan, two other kids from the lacrosse team who were also part of the superathlete club at school. Chad saw me and waved.

"I'm going to Chad's house for a barbecue, remember?"

Daisy shook her head. "I don't get it. It seems like this is happening a lot."

"What is?"

"You being too busy to do stuff with us," Irwin chimed in.

"That's totally not fair," I said, my voice rising a little bit. "Just because I'm on the lacrosse team now doesn't mean I'm not still best friends with you guys. But I just can't do everything anytime you want."

"That's lame," Irwin said.

"It's not lame!" I snapped. "Maybe you should join something so you're not just sitting around all day waiting for me to come play with you to solve some fake case that nobody cares about."

Irwin's face turned red, like he'd been stung by a bee. He hadn't, though. He'd been stung by a friend. Me.

"I didn't mean it like that," I told him, but he wouldn't look at me. I turned to Daisy. "I didn't mean it like that," I said again. But she just shook her head.

"Being on the lacrosse team takes up a ton of time," said Baxter. "Neither one of us will be around very much for a while. That's just the way it is."

Baxter coming to my defense made me feel *really* lousy about yelling at him during the game.

"That's just the way it is, huh?" Irwin said. "Well, Baxter, that's pretty funny coming from you. The only reason you're even in this club is because we felt sorry for you."

Baxter looked like he'd been punched in the stomach.

"That's not fair, Irwin," I said. "Knock it off."

"FINE," Irwin hollered, getting on his bike. "I'm leaving!"

"I'm leaving too," Baxter said softly. "This isn't fun any-more." And he walked away without looking at any of us.

Mara looked shocked. The gang that she wanted to join five minutes earlier was dissolving right before her

very eyes. "Um, I'm going to go talk to some other kids," she said finally.

That left Daisy and me, standing there with nothing to say to each other. After we won the game I'd felt as good as I'd ever felt in my life. Now it seemed like the world was crashing down all around me.

"What do we do now?" I said to Daisy.

"I don't know," she said back. "I guess maybe the gang should break up. Just for a while until everything gets back to normal."

I suddenly felt a little nauseous. "When's that going to be?"

But Daisy just shook her head and said, "I don't know."

I felt a smack on my shoulder, and I turned around to see Chad standing there. "Ready to roll?" Chad asked. "You got everything you need?"

I looked around at my teammates, at my parents, and finally at Daisy, who was staring at me with a confused expression on her face.

"Yeah," I said finally. "I got everything I need."

CHAPTER 20

GOING TO CHAD'S HOUSE was like exploring a distant planet that I'd heard about for years but never thought I'd get to visit in person. It's a planet where everyone is good at sports, and where everyone proves they're best friends by wrestling, punching each other on the shoulder, and throwing each other to the ground. And it's a planet where people seem really, really happy, because they got really lucky in life and they know it.

"Jimmy, welcome!" said Chad's mom, a woman whose skin looked like the tan couch in our living room. "Help yourself to a snack before lunch!"

"I will, thanks, Mrs. Knight."

Chad yanked my arm. "Let's go outside and play hoops."

"Hoops?"

"Basketball."

"Oh, right."

The last time I'd felt comfortable playing basketball was when I was about five years old, and it involved a squishy orange ball and a tiny rim. My lack of skill didn't matter, though, because the basketball game turned out to be just an excuse for kids to wrestle, grab, and peg the ball at each other as hard as they could. I seemed to be the only one who was terrified, though—everyone else was having the time of their lives.

Luckily, Mrs. Knight yelled "LUNCH!" before anybody got killed.

As the hot dogs (yummy) and cheeseburgers (yummier) were served and scarfed down, Coach Knight got up to make a toast.

"Congratulations to the boys from the lacrosse team," he said, nodding in the direction of our picnic table, where I was sitting with Chad, his big brother, Jarrod (Misty's boyfriend), and our teammates Eric and Stefan. "They played a great game today, overcame a fluke accident at halftime, and beat a really good team. Some solid offense by the guys up front. And that last-second save by Jimmy Bishop was one for the highlight reel. Way to go, boys!"

Everyone cheered, and we all stood up and waved. I felt like I was running for president or something, but I wasn't. All I was doing was playing goalie on a fifth-grade lacrosse team.

FACT: If you think adults are intense about adult sports, you should see how they are about *youth* sports.

A little while later, I was diving into an ice cream sandwich when Coach Knight came up behind me and said, "How's everything, Jimmy? You having a good time?"

"Absolutely, Coach."

"Terrific," he said. "Listen, I want to talk to you a bit about the future."

I looked up at him, confused. "What about it?"

Coach sat down. "Well, it's no secret that we've been having some real problems with our field, and with our program. This whole season it's been like a war zone out there, with open storm drains and rotting benches. The parents are worried, and personally, I just can't continue to coach under these conditions. It's time for me to step things up to the next level." He paused for a minute, and

I realized he actually seemed a little nervous. "That's what I wanted to talk to you about. I've decided that next year, I'll be joining the LaxMax program."

I was shocked. LaxMax, our archrival? All Coach Knight ever talked about was beating them in the championship. Now he was going to join their program?

"You hate them!" I reminded Coach.

"I know, I know," he said. "But I figure, if you can't beat 'em, join 'em." Coach smiled. "Even though we *are* going to whup them this year."

"Wow," I said. "I can't believe it."

Coach Knight took a sip of his drink. "I know, it's crazy. But LaxMax is an elite program, Jimmy, not just a town program. And they're always looking for the best new coaches and players. Chad is going to join the junior team, and I'm going to join their coaching staff." He put his hand on my shoulder and smiled. "That's what I wanted to talk to you about. I'm hoping you'll consider coming with us."

I looked over at Chad. "You're joining LaxMax too?"

He shrugged. "Looks that way."

"I've already told the head of the LaxMax program about you," Coach Knight said. "They're always looking for good goalies. And you're getting better every game."

I started to feel that warm glow you get when someone tells you you're good at something.

"This is big news, Jimmy, I promise you," said Coach Knight. "Very exciting, for all of us."

"What about the rest of the guys, though?" I asked. "We're a team."

Coach sighed. "I know. It's a little unfortunate. There just isn't enough money in the budget for Quietville to stay competitive in this day and age. Just ask that bench that broke!" He got up. "Anyway, it's something to think about. Talk it over with your parents, and we'll discuss it more in the coming weeks. For now, we still have the rest of this season, and we still want to win a championship!"

As Coach Knight walked away, Chad took a sip of his soda.

"Can I tell you something?" he asked. "Kind of a secret?"

"Sure."

"I don't even like lacrosse that much."

I was shocked. "What? You don't? You're amazing at it."

"I guess." He started making smiley faces out of the leftover ketchup on his plate. "But sometimes I wish I wasn't."

"Wow. That's crazy."

"Not that crazy," he said. "I like basketball better. But my dad says I'm not tall enough for basketball, and since I'm so good at lacrosse I need to play it all year round."

"Huh," I said, thinking about my dad and how thrilled he was that I was turning out to be a good lacrosse player. "Well, I guess joining LaxMax will mean a much better field, right? I don't get why we can't get a decent field here, and benches that actually work. Especially since kids are getting hurt! Is it really that much of a big deal?"

"I guess so," Chad said. "That's why we need to go to LaxMax, right? They're the best."

"You think I'm really good enough for them?" I asked him.

"Yeah, I do," he said. "It's pretty awesome how quickly you got so good."

"Thanks." It *was* awesome. So why didn't I *feel* awesome?

He held out his hand for a high five, and we slapped palms. "Listen, it's all good, right? This is gonna be sweet. You're one of us now!"

And I realized, *Maybe that's the problem.*

I didn't really feel like one of us.

Or one of them.

Or one of anybody.

PART TWO

BAD NEWS

IN THE BOOK *FANGS BUT NO FANGS*, Jonah Forrester wakes up one morning and has completely lost his vampire powers. He freaks out at first, because everything he knows is gone. But then, slowly, he gets used to it, and actually enjoys being a normal person. He decides that not having all the complications of being a vampire is actually a lot easier, and he convinces himself he's happier than ever, until the day he realizes something: He misses his old life.

I kind of knew how Jonah felt.

After the CrimeBiters broke up, a couple of strange things happened. The first was awesome: Not to brag or anything, but Chad was right—I was getting pretty amazing at lacrosse. Our team kept winning, we made the playoffs, and the team named me a co-captain with Chad.

But the other strange thing was the opposite of awesome: Three more kids on our team got injured in weird accidents on our home field. In our game against Fairfield, Alex Kaplan tripped over an old telephone wire that was sticking up from the ground; and in the game against Eastchester, two kids got hurt: Kenny Stephensen banged into one of the goals when it came loose, and Nick Wingate slipped and twisted his ankle when the sprinklers went off in the middle of the third quarter.

Watching Nick get helped off the field, I found myself standing next to Baxter.

"Hey, can I ask you something?"

He looked at me like I was about to ask him to eat an entire plate of brussels sprouts in five seconds. "Sure, I guess."

"Does this always happen? Kids getting hurt like this?"

Baxter chuckled a little. "Why, you nervous?"

"No, of course not," I said. "I just think it's weird, that's all. Don't you?"

He shrugged. "Kids get hurt in sports all the time."

"Well, how come no one ever gets hurt when we play away games?"

"Because our field stinks, duh." Baxter snorted.

"Listen, you're lucky you're not playing football. It's way worse."

"Huh," I said, trying to believe him. I was no expert, but I was pretty sure that kids didn't get hurt in football with telephone wires. I decided not to make a big deal out of it. "Okay," I said. "Thanks."

I was still a little nervous about the whole thing, but there weren't any injuries for the next few games, and everything seemed to calm down. I soon got distracted by something else, anyway: About halfway through our winning streak, a bunch of kids on the team started asking me and Chad if we were going to join LaxMax. I didn't know where they heard that rumor, but I pretended not to know what they were talking about. That was because after I'd told my parents about the conversation I'd had with Coach Knight, my dad said (with an incredibly proud look on his face), "That's not something you should even think about until after the season is over. Right now your focus needs to be on your team."

Got it. Focus!

FACT: Always put the team's needs ahead of your own. Except when you're alone, lying in bed at night. Then it's perfectly fine to dream about personal glory.

CHAPTER 22

MEANWHILE, while all the injury stuff with lacrosse was pretty strange, something way stranger was going on: Abby was turning into the most perfectly behaved dog who ever lived. At obedience class, she was the first one to finish all the exercises. At home, she hadn't used my mom's shoes for a between-meal snack in weeks. She kept ignoring Mrs. Cragg's coffin-bed, and she never ever EVER snuck out of my bedroom window anymore.

Every night before bed, we'd go through the same sad routine. I'd fish Abby's usual toys out of the closet: an old slipper, a small towel, and a sock that she'd stolen a few months earlier.

She'd look at the toys, then back at me.

"You may play," I would say.

She'd play with the old slipper for a minute, then look back up at me.

"You may continue to play," I would say. And Abby would.

This would usually go on for about twenty minutes: Every thirty seconds, Abby would look at me for permission to continue playing. It was a little ridiculous.

"I must point out how well-mannered Abby has become," my mom said one night at dinner, the night after our game against Eastchester. Abby was sleeping peacefully at my feet. "No begging at all."

"She's really turned it around," my dad agreed.

"Did you trick her or something?" Misty asked me. "I know how you like to sneak her a big bone sometimes."

I kicked Misty under the table.

"Ow!" she said. "Well, did you?"

"I didn't! That's the crazy thing. She's being good all by herself."

"I have a feeling this whole dog thing is going to work out after all," my dad said. My parents smiled at each other. They were so happy that the obedience training was really working.

That made two of them.

"I do kind of miss seeing her fangs," I couldn't help saying. "They are kind of awesome."

"Some fangs are better left unseen," my dad said. Then he cracked up, like he'd made some sort of joke, even though I had no idea what it was.

Later that night, I finally couldn't take it anymore. I looked down at Abby, lying peacefully on a sweatshirt in my closet (the coffin-shaped bed sat there unused, as usual), and I decided to do an experiment. I jumped up suddenly, like I'd seen something scary. Then I ran to the open window and yelled, "Whoa! What was that?"

But Abby just sat there, looking completely relaxed. She wasn't even on high alert.

"I saw something out there, Ab!" I said. "Go find out what it was." But she didn't move.

I took her little head in my hands. "Oh, Abby," I said. "What if it really had been something scary? Then what? I need to know if you're the special dog I thought you were!" But she didn't answer—probably because she was a dog.

"Think about big Thor!" I urged. "You know he'd be out there going nuts, digging holes and tearing up the place! Doesn't that sound like fun?"

Still, nothing.

Finally, I decided to take matters into my own hands.

"Okay, let's go." I threw on my slippers and we headed outside. It was a pitch-black night, just the way she liked it—but not exactly the way I liked it. "I'm going to wait here by the door," I told Abby. "Go do your thing." But she didn't go do her thing. Instead she sat at attention, looking directly at me and waiting for her next instruction, exactly the way Shep had taught her.

"Fine, be that way," I said. "Let's go visit Herman." Abby and Herman the groundhog liked to challenge each other with all sorts of vicious noises and growls and threats.

We walked over to Herman's hole, and Abby looked down. But instead of frantically trying to dig her way to the bottom, she just lay down on top of it.

"Oh, jeez," I said. "Don't tell me you like Herman now."

After about five more minutes, I gave up. "Good dog," I said. And we went inside to bed.

FACT: Sometimes "Good dog" isn't necessarily a compliment.

That night, I had a weird dream: Abby was back to her old self, and she was growling and prowling and was just about to sink her giant fangs into the arm of a bad guy. I was so excited. But then the bad guy turned around and it was . . . Coach Knight! Oh no! "Abby!" I yelled. "What have you done?!?" My parents were yelling, "That's it! She's going right back to the shelter!"

Yikes.

I woke up in a cold sweat. Maybe Abby being normal was a good thing after all.

THE NEXT DAY, my parents told me the good news: They'd decided that Abby was now well-behaved enough to come to our first playoff game.

"Isn't that awesome?" my dad asked.

"Yup!" I said, throwing in the exclamation point to try and sound like I meant it.

At the game, Abby sat in the stands quietly, snoozing under the bench and minding her own business. During halftime my dad quietly walked her around the field, where people petted her, she said hi to a few other dogs, and she sniffed a few flowers and trees. Coach was giving us his usual pep talk (on our new, metal bench), but I wasn't listening. Instead I was watching Abby and realizing something kind of sad. I was officially starting to doubt that Abby had special powers after all. I might have been imagining the whole thing. The proof was right there before my very eyes.

Abby had become just like every other dog.

Meanwhile, in the first quarter, another kid on our team got hurt: The netting on Kyle Shuken's stick turned out to have a hole in it, and he got hit in the face with the ball. Luckily, it was just a bruise, but he had to leave the game.

"There's no way you can tell me this would happen in a football game," I said to Baxter.

Baxter looked like he wasn't in the mood to listen to the new star goalie complain. "Listen, Jimmy, if you're so worried about getting hurt, you should just quit," he said. "No one's forcing you to play, you know."

Even though Kyle was one of our best defenders, we still managed to win the game, 5–3. That meant we were going to play LaxMax in the district championship. Go, us! I hugged my family and Abby, and all the parents and people who watched the game were patting me on the back and telling me how great I was. Everyone was so excited, and I tried to be excited too, but something didn't feel right.

It almost felt like the more everyone treated me like I was special, the more I wanted to go back to normal. And the more normal Abby got, the more I wanted her to go back to being special.

My mom, of course, was the only one who could tell. (Even though she works a lot, she's still my mom.) "What's wrong, honey?" she asked as I sat on the bench taking my equipment off.

"Nothing!" I insisted, but I think we both knew that wasn't true.

I missed my old gang.

I missed my old friends.

I missed my old vampire dog.

I missed my old life.

A FEW DAYS LATER, I walked into the house and tossed down my backpack. "Hello? Anybody home?"

"In here!"

Mrs. Cragg was in the kitchen, humming along to the radio. Abby was snoozing under the table. "Well, hello there, Jimmy!"

"Oh, hi. I didn't know you were babysitting."

She laughed. "Chauffeuring is the correct term, I believe. Don't you need some rides today?"

I sat down at the table and shrugged. "I don't think so."

"Are you sure? Your dad told me you did. What happened to that very busy schedule of yours?"

I shrugged again.

Mrs. Cragg sat down next to me. "Is everything okay, Jimmy?"

I thought about telling her the truth—*Well, I've been spending a lot of time missing my best friends and wishing we'd become a gang again, but that's not possible because I kind of acted like a jerk, and tomorrow is the lacrosse championship but I don't really want to play because it's not fun anymore and all I can think about is how I messed everything up with the CrimeBiters*—but then I decided to go with "Sure, I guess."

Mrs. Cragg smiled. "Well, then I'm glad for the company."

"What are you making?"

"What does it smell like?"

I took a deep whiff. The smell of deliciousness was overpowering. "Muffins."

"Correct! Chocolate banana muffins, to be exact. Would you like to try one?"

"Oh, no, it's okay, thanks anyway," I said, which really meant *One would be good, but seven would be better.*

FACT: Chocolate banana muffins can really pick a guy up when he's down.

She laughed and put a muffin in front of me. "You've turned into such a polite young man." She looked at Abby. "And your little dog here has become a total sweetheart."

"Thanks," I said, between bites. "She's great, I guess. I kind of wish she was a little more like she used to be, though."

"Oh, don't you worry," Mrs. Cragg said. "When you need her to be, she'll be right there, protecting you every step of the way."

I looked at Abby, snoozing away. It seemed hard to believe that she could protect anybody. "If you say so," I said.

"I do say so," Mrs. Cragg said. "So what will you do today? Are you going to meet your friends? Don't you have lacrosse practice?"

I avoided her eyes. "Not today," I lied. "I think I'll just watch some TV or something."

Mrs. Cragg frowned. "I thought you said you didn't really do that anymore."

"I decided I missed it."

"I see."

She watched me chew for a second, then said, "I hear you're very good at lacrosse."

I shrugged. "Kind of, I guess. We're doing really well. Kids keep getting injured, though. It's weird."

Mrs. Cragg frowned. "Weird how?"

"Well, our field is really bad, and a bunch of times during the season, some kid has gotten hurt in some fluke-y way. Then, at our last game, a kid's stick had a hole in it, and he got hit in the face with the ball. He's got, like, a huge black eye."

"Yikes," Mrs. Cragg said. "It almost sounds like someone has it out for you guys."

I looked at her. "Really? Like who?"

She shook her head. "Oh, I don't really mean it, Jimmy. It just sounds like an awful streak of bad luck, that's all."

"I guess." But I thought about what she said. Could it be true?

Mrs. Cragg handed me a glass of milk, which I finished in one gulp. "Is everything else all right?" she asked.

"Oh, sure," I said. "Except my friends all hate me."

"I'm sure that's not true."

"Or should I say, ex-friends."

She sighed. "You know, Jimmy, sometimes people just act kind of funny. They can't help it."

"What do you mean?"

"I mean that for some strange reason, people act the worst to the people they're closest with. It's almost like, if you're good friends with someone, you're comfortable enough to behave badly around them. Bratty, even."

I tried to laugh. "Maybe that's why my sister always acts like a complete nightmare around me."

"Exactly!" Mrs. Cragg refilled my glass. "But eventually, if you're good friends, you'll find a way to forgive each other. It just takes someone to make the first move." She paused. "Perhaps that someone could be you."

I thought about that for a second. "Maybe I will go to the clubhouse," I said. "Just for a little while."

Mrs. Cragg smiled. "Do you want a muffin for the road?"

I took two.

CHAPTER 24

BUT MY FRIENDS WEREN'T AT THE CLUBHOUSE.

Nobody was.

It was just me and Abby, sitting at the broken-down picnic table.

The only sound you could hear was the occasional bullfrog clearing its throat.

"Let's go up top," I told Abby. We went up the old stairs in the back of the building, and went to the roof, where we held most of our CrimeBiters meetings. The big hole in the floorboards was still there. I stared at it, remembering the moment when Baxter's dad had us cornered, until Irwin and I outsmarted him and tricked him into falling through the rotted wood all the way to the floor below. That was the moment the CrimeBiters gang was born.

"Some things are worth fighting for . . . but justice is worth biting for," I murmured to myself. It was Jonah Forrester's catchphrase, and I used to shout it from the roof all the time, when Irwin and I went to the Boathouse every day after school.

Those days seemed like a long time ago.

I took out my copy of *Fangs but No Fangs* and was just sitting down to read, when I heard the rickety screen door slam downstairs, then footsteps.

They came! Daisy and Irwin must have gone to my house, and Mrs. Cragg must have told them I was here, and they came to make up! They would say I'm sorry, and then I would say I'm sorry, and we could go back to how it was before!

I ran downstairs to greet them, yelling, "Hello? Anybody here?" I jumped off the last step and saw Baxter standing there. He was totally out of breath and wearing his lacrosse stuff.

"Jimmy! There you are! I've been looking all over for you."

"If you're here because you want the CrimeBiters to get back together, well, so do I," I said. "I don't think it's going to work with just the two of us, though, so we may as well forget it."

Baxter shook his head. "That's not why I'm here, and you know it."

"Oh," I said.

"You're skipping practice?"

I didn't say anything.

"What, you want to quit lacrosse or something?" Baxter added.

I didn't realize it until that second, but I think maybe I did.

He was staring at me, and I knew I couldn't avoid the topic forever. "I actually don't think I'm going to go to practice today."

Baxter's eyes went wide with disbelief. "Are you serious? What is wrong with you? It's our last practice. The championship game is tomorrow!!"

"Yeah, well, I don't know. Lacrosse isn't fun anymore. It's too intense, you know? Too many kids are getting hurt. Your aunt Agnes said it's almost like someone is out to get us."

Baxter's face turned red, and I realized that I'd never referred to Mrs. Cragg as his aunt before.

"Do you think it's possible, Baxter?" I said, trying to take his mind off that stuff. "That someone is hurting the kids on our team on purpose?"

"I suppose anything's possible," Baxter said. "People take this stuff way too seriously. But it's crazy too. Who would do that?"

"I agree," I said. "It's crazy." We sat there for another minute, then I said, "I wonder what Daisy and Irwin would think."

Neither one of us had to add that we couldn't find out, since they weren't there.

"All I know," Baxter said, "is that our team needs you. We're playing LaxMax tomorrow!"

"They'll kill us," I moaned.

"Not this time! Not with you in the goal! And we've never beaten those guys!"

"That would be sweet," I agreed.

"So, you in? Come on, we're late!"

Woof! Woof! I looked down at Abby, whose tail was standing straight up. She looked like she was trying to tell me something. She looked like she was trying to tell me, *Stop feeling sorry for yourself.*

"Okay," I said. "I'm in."

COACH KNIGHT SEEMED HAPPY and relieved to see me. Well, sure, yeah, he blew his whistle and barked, "You're late, take ten laps!" at me when I got there, but he was smiling when he said it.

On my fifth lap, Chad came over and started running next to me. "What happened? Where were you?"

"I had some stuff I had to figure out."

"Was it with your friends? The CrimeBiters kids?"

I stopped. "You know about that?"

"Of course," Chad said. "I used to hear you guys talk about it in school all the time. You're like a club, right? It sounds totally fun."

Whoa.

I tried not to look too shocked that the best athlete in the grade was curious about the CrimeBiters, so instead I just shrugged. "Well, yeah, except we're not actually a club anymore right now. We kind of broke up."

"Really? That stinks. I wish I had a gang like that to hang around with." Chad pointed at Eric and Stefan, two kids on the team who were passing a ball back and forth. "Those guys are okay, but all they do is talk about sports all the time. It gets kind of boring after a while."

I stared at him. "Um . . . okay . . . if we get back together I'll let you know."

Chad smacked me on the helmet—luckily, not as hard as his dad.

"Cool. Thanks."

FACT: Kids can really surprise you sometimes.

PRACTICE WAS ALMOST OVER when things started to go wrong.

We were all running to our sideline to take a water break when Jeremy Vandroff fell awkwardly and scraped his knee. "What was that?" he mumbled to the rest of us, sitting on the bench and putting a paper towel on his leg to stop the bleeding. "I was just running along and then I fell for no reason!"

Coach Knight hurried over to take a look. "You're fine," he said to Jeremy. "No swelling. You can take a break or get back in there, up to you." Jeremy immediately jumped up and put his helmet back on.

FACT: There are absolutely no weenies allowed in sports.

"Okay, let's go!" Coach hollered. "Pick it up! Finish strong! Big game tomorrow!" We started the drill again, but five minutes later, I heard another scream.

"OOOOWWW!"

Somebody was lying on the ground, but I couldn't tell who it was, because everyone had crowded around. "Give him room!" Coach Knight was yelling. "Give him room!"

I ran over and looked to see who it was.

Chad.

Uh-oh.

He was lying there, rubbing his leg. "Holy smokes, that kills," he said. His dad was kneeling next to him, applying an ice pack, saying, "You'll be fine, son."

"What happened?" I asked Chad's friend Eric, who was standing next to him.

Eric shook his head. "I have no idea. All I know is that one minute he was running right next to me, and the next, he was on the ground, screaming in pain."

Jeremy Vandroff looked scared. "That's right near where I fell."

I suddenly got a really bad feeling in my stomach. It was scary enough that kids were getting hurt in games. But in *practice?!?*

Coach Knight stood up. "Okay, boys, bring it in! Gather around!" We formed a tight circle around him. "That's enough for today. Let's knock off a little early, so everyone can go home and get some rest. We all know this is a lousy field, but the good news is we're playing on the high school field tomorrow, so no more bad surprises." He looked down at his son, who was still sitting on the ground, putting ice on his ankle. Boy, Chad was a tough kid. If it had been me, I'd be bawling my eyes out.

"We're going to try to get Chad ready for tomorrow's game," Coach continued. "If he can play, he will. But if he can't, I don't want the rest of you to hang your heads. We can beat LaxMax, with or without Chad! I mean it! Victory on three!"

He counted "One, two, three," and we all screamed "Victory!"

After practice I walked up to the parking lot, where I saw Baxter sitting on a bench, staring into space.

"See?" I said to him. "Two more kids getting hurt. And in practice!"

"All I know is we're going to get killed tomorrow if Chad can't play," Baxter said. "We may as well not even show up."

I stared at him. "Hold on a second. Aren't you the one who told me that I had to come to practice, that we were a team, and quitters were losers?"

"That was before Chad got hurt," he said.

"We stick together, no matter what!"

Baxter laughed sadly. "Whatever."

I didn't really have anything to say to that, so we sat there quietly, waiting for our rides.

It was probably about five more minutes, but it felt like an hour.

CHAPTER 27

IT WAS THE LAST NIGHT OF OBEDIENCE TRAINING, so my parents decided to come with me.

"Are they planning anything special?" my mom asked in the car.

I stared out the window. "I think there's, like, a graduation ceremony or something."

"That sounds like fun!"

"Whatever."

"Someone's in a mood," said my dad, glancing back at me.

I sighed. He was right, I *was* in a mood, and it wasn't a very good one. My gang was disbanded, my dog was just like any dog, and we were going to get killed by LaxMax the very next day. Can you blame me?

My mom turned the radio down. "Do you want to talk about it?"

"Not really." I looked over at Abby, calmly licking her

169

paws. She looked like she didn't have a care in the world. Good for her!

FACT: Sometimes I wish I were a dog.

As we parked the car, my dad said, "Try to cheer up and have some fun!"

"Think of how far Abby has come," my mom added. "The entire shoe community can finally breathe a sigh of relief."

I tried to laugh, but it didn't work.

Inside the shelter, Shep came over to greet us. "Hey, Mr. and Mrs. Bishop," he said to my parents. "Jimmy has really done a great job with Abby. She's, like, the mellowest dog in the world now. She's practically unrecognizable."

Yeah, that's the problem, I said to myself.

While my parents were chatting with some of the other dog owners, Shep pulled me aside. "Hey, dude. I know you're not loving this new version of your dog. But I've been around dogs a long time, and trust me, they are who they are."

I looked at him. "What does that mean?"

He winked. "It means Abby will always be Abby."

Before I could even think about what that meant, Shep clapped his hands together. "Okay, people! It's time for the Big Kahuna. The last roundup! The final exam!"

Everyone started murmuring with excitement as we all formed a circle and Shep began putting each dog through their paces.

"Sit."

"Paw."

"Fetch."

"Drag and drop."

"Bury the bone."

"Weave." (That's where the dog walks in between your legs three times.)

"Circle." (That's where the dog walks around their owner three times.)

"Leave it." (That's where Shep puts a biscuit on the floor but the dog doesn't move.)

"Take it." (That's where the dog is allowed to eat the biscuit.)

"Follow your star."

"Rest."

"Lie down."

"Stand up."

Then, for the last trick—no wait, Shep says they're not tricks, they're "canine enrichment exercises"—he put a ball next to a wall with four holes in it, and the dogs were supposed to nudge the ball through the first hole, run around the other side to put the ball back through the second hole, and do the same thing again for the third and fourth holes. Then the dog nudges the ball back to Shep.

After each dog did all the exercises correctly, Shep clipped a blue dog tag onto their collar and said, "Congratulations. You are now a graduate of the Northport ARF's Dandy Dog Program—and an *ARFULLY* good dog!" And everyone cheered while the dogs proudly wagged their tails.

Shep worked his way around the circle and got through most of the dogs—there were Stella, Bailey, Theo, Woody, and two dogs whose names I forgot—and then walked up to Abby. So far, all the dogs had passed with flying colors.

"Well, hello there, missy," Shep said to Abby. "Are you ready to strut your stuff?"

Abby stared up at him, completely still. She looked

like the most obedient dog in the world. And even though I liked her better the way she was before, I still felt pretty proud.

"Sit."

"Paw."

"Fetch."

"Weave."

"Circle."

Abby was halfway through her second circle when the door opened. In came Thor and Mr. Swab.

"Sorry we're late," Mr. Swab told Shep. "A lot going on. Big day tomorrow."

"What's tomorrow?" I asked, but he'd already turned to shake hands with my parents. "Hello there. Exciting night, huh? May the best dog win."

"Uh, I don't think it's a competition," my mom answered.

"*Everything* is a competition," Mr. Swab said. "It's a dog-eat-dog world, haven't you heard? Especially in here!" He laughed at his own joke.

Thor and Abby had a happy reunion, nipping and playing and barking. Mr. Swab bent down to pet Abby. Then Thor romped around saying hi to all the dogs, and as usual I got a little jealous over how high-spirited he was, compared to my mellow little girl.

"How are you tonight, little pooch?" Mr. Swab said to Abby. "Your usual perfect self?"

And that's the moment I saw something I hadn't seen in a very long time.

Abby's fangs.

She gave out a quiet little growl, and I saw the fangs flash.

"Abby!" I said. After all these weeks of perfect (or perfectly boring) behavior, the last thing I needed was for her to blow it at the graduation, in front of my parents.

At first, I was pretty sure that I was the only one who noticed the growl and the fangs, but I was wrong.

Thor did too.

FACT: Dogs are very protective of their owners. And the same goes for the other way around.

Thor came over, the hair on his back sticking straight up. He sniffed Abby—*don't try anything*—and Abby backed away.

Mr. Swab chuckled. "Well, there you go. Seems like your dog knows a size difference when she sees one."

I nodded. "It wouldn't be a fair fight, that's for sure."

"Yup. Better tell your little dog there to keep your distance!" Mr. Swab gave me a smack on the back for emphasis.

Well, maybe there was something Abby didn't like about that smack, because that was all it took.

"AWOOOO!" Abby howled at the top of her lungs. Then she started running around in a circle, making strange noises, and barking her head off at Mr. Swab.

"Abby, what are you doing?" I cried.

"There's something really wrong with your dog," said Mr. Swab, looking smug because someone else's dog was causing trouble for once. "Guess she's not a straight-A student after all!"

My parents and I tried to grab Abby, but she was too quick.

"It's like her tail is on fire," said Shep, who looked kind of amused by the whole thing.

Finally, as Abby jumped out of my reach, Mr. Swab grabbed her from behind. She turned around, saw who was holding her, and went full fang.

"GRRRRGGHHH!"

Abby looked like she was just about to chomp on Mr. Swab's nose when he had the good sense to drop her. I snatched her up and clipped the leash on her collar. She was still all wound up, panting and growling.

"ABBY, THAT'S ENOUGH!" I hollered.

"That dog is crazy!" exclaimed Mr. Swab, scrambling out of the way. "She almost took my face off! She needs to be locked up!"

"Oh, for crying out loud," Shep said. But he did look a little upset by Abby's behavior. As did everyone else.

Thor, meanwhile, decided to show Abby what a *real* growl was like, and since he weighed about a hundred pounds more than Abby, he had a good point.

"GRRRRGGGHH!"

This time, Abby didn't back down at all. Abby and Thor just stared at each other, waiting for the other to make the first move.

"Sit!" I hollered.

"Stay!" my dad hollered.

"Follow your star!" Shep hollered, for no apparent reason.

As Mr. Swab pulled Thor away, I noticed something flash off his chest. At first, I couldn't quite tell what it was, but then I saw it, clear as day.

"That's it!" I announced. "Look!"

"What's it?" my mom said.

I pointed at Mr. Swab's chest. "He's wearing a cross around his neck!"

Everyone stared at me as if I had two heads.

"So what?" said my dad sensibly.

"Everyone knows that a cross—" But I stopped myself.

I was about to say *Everyone knows that a cross is the one thing besides garlic that a vampire hates*, but then I realized, *That would make me seem like a crazy person, even to myself. Abby hasn't done anything vampire-ish since, like, forever.*

"What about a cross?" asked my dad.

I shook my head. "Nothing."

FACT: Sometimes it's better to keep your vampirical thoughts to yourself.

Mr. Swab, meanwhile, was walking Thor to the door. "You better fail that dog, Shep!" he said, pointing at Abby.

Shep rolled his eyes. "There are no grades in this class."

"I'm so sorry," my mom kept saying to anyone who would listen. "Abby is a little unpredictable."

"No, she's not!" I protested. "She's gotten completely predictable! Too predictable!"

Shep shook his head. "Actually, the one thing predictable about dogs is that they're never predictable."

"It's like we're right back at square one," my dad said, sounding pretty mad. "We can't have a dog that might fly off the handle at any time, for absolutely no reason. It's too dangerous. We could get sued, for crying out loud!"

My mom sighed. "Let's go," she said. "We'll talk about it more at home."

As we walked to the parking lot, I wanted to scream. But instead, I just looked down at Abby.

"Why did you have to do that?" I asked her. "I know you hate crosses, but so what? You're making it really, really hard on me, you know that?"

Abby didn't answer.

Instead, she weaved through my legs perfectly, the whole way to the car.

CHAPTER 28

SO, AS IT TURNS OUT, a little excitement and one cross was all it took.

Abby was back to her old self.

The first thing she did when she got home was jump into the coffin-looking bed that Mrs. Cragg had given her. She'd never even gone near it before! But that night, she snuggled right in.

Then, while Misty was doing homework (but really mostly texting Jarrod) in the TV room, Abby started staring out the window, on high alert, scanning the neighborhood for anything suspicious.

"What's she looking for?" Misty asked.

"Bad guys," I answered. Misty rolled her eyes, but I ignored her.

That was the good news.

The bad news was, my parents and I were having another one of those *talks*.

"We've tried, Jimmy," said my mom. "We really have."

"I want to keep her just as much as you do," said my dad. "But at a certain point, you have to wonder if this is really the place for her."

My mom nodded in agreement. "Maybe she needs a home where she can run free outside all day long, away from people and other things that might get her in trouble."

I just looked back at them. I know they were expecting me to put up a fight, just like always, but this time, I was silent. I just didn't have it in me, I guess. And besides, what was I going to say? Abby randomly went a little crazy, just because some guy who happened to have an annoying personality was wearing a cross around his neck? That wasn't going to work, vampire or no vampire.

"Can I just ask one thing?" I said finally.

My mom smiled. "Sure, honey."

"Can Abby come to the game tomorrow night? It's the championship, and I want her there for luck. Then we can figure out what to do after it's over. Okay?"

My parents looked at each other. My mom's eyes were saying no, but my dad's eyes were saying yes. Luckily, my dad's eyes won.

"Fine," he said. "But she stays on her leash the whole time."

I breathed a sigh of relief. For some reason, I had a weird feeling that as long as Abby could come to the game, everything would work out okay.

Later that night, I opened the window before I went to bed, even though Abby hadn't gone for a night walk for weeks. I'd barely had the window open for a second before Abby darted through.

Things were back to normal!

In other words, totally abnormal.

CHAPTER 29

THE NEXT DAY AT LUNCH, I went looking for the other CrimeBiters, since we didn't usually sit together anymore.

I found Irwin first. "Just thought you might want to know that Abby is back to her old self," I told him.

"Okay," Irwin said, with a face that said, *Why would you think I'd care?*

But then I added, "I'm going to go find Daisy, since she loves Abby and I think she might want to know."

Which made Irwin stand up and say, "I'll come with you."

FACT: Old habits die hard. Or—as in the case of Irwin making sure I don't ever have a conversation with Daisy without him—they never die at all.

The two of us went over to Daisy's table. She was sitting with Mara Lloyd and some little kid I didn't recognize.

"Hey!" Daisy said. "This is Devon. He's in second grade, and he and Mara have become friends."

I looked at Devon, then at Mara. "Don't tell me *he's* your secret admirer."

"Yes!" Mara said happily. "Isn't it adorable? We found him thanks to Daisy and Irwin! Your gang is awesome. If you guys ever get back together, I totally want to join!"

Devon was sitting there, slurping his chocolate milk, gazing at Mara. This little boy was the cause of all our arguments? This was the kid who broke up the CrimeBiters?

I almost couldn't believe it.

"Well, that's great," I said, looking at Mara. "I hope you two will be very happy together." I turned back to Daisy. "Anyway, I just wanted to let you know that Abby is back to her old self."

"Hurray!" Daisy said. Then she looked across the cafeteria. "Did you tell Irwin and Baxter?"

"Just Irwin so far," I said.

"I think you should tell Baxter too," Daisy said. "Irwin and I will come with you."

I tried to play it casual, even though my heart was racing. "Fine."

The three of us walked over to Baxter's table. "Abby is back to her old self," I told him.

"That's great," Baxter said.

We all looked at each other for a minute, awkwardly. No one said anything. But still, we were all together. It was a start, at least.

Finally, Irwin said, "Exactly what do you mean, back to her old self?"

"She showed her fangs last night and went on a night patrol."

They looked at me blankly.

"She almost bit Mr. Swab," I added. "The guy who takes his dog to the same obedience class I go to."

"Is he a bad person?" said Daisy. "Did he deserve to get bitten?"

Oh right, that.

"Uh . . ." I began, trying to think of what to say. "Well, he's really annoying sometimes."

"Yeah, that doesn't count," Baxter said. The three of them stared at me.

"That's not the point!" I said. "The point is, Abby is back! I feel like it's a sign that the gang should get back together too, right? Especially since lacrosse season ends after tonight's game!"

"Abby can't just bite people," Baxter said.

"I know!" I said. "That's why we need to meet! My parents are thinking about taking her back to the shelter! Again!"

"That stinks," Daisy said.

Irwin finally nodded. "Okay, fine. Maybe we can meet at my house after the game and plan our next move. Figure out how Jimmy can keep Abby."

"I'm in," Baxter said.

"Thanks, you guys," I said, relieved.

We all turned to Daisy.

"I can't."

I dropped a fork I didn't realize I'd been holding.

She looked a little embarrassed. "I told Mara I'd go to the movies with her tonight."

My heart started to race. In the back of my mind, I'd always wondered why Daisy was a CrimeBiter. It was only a matter of time before she found other people that she wanted to hang around with more than us. But now that it had officially happened, I wasn't quite sure how to react.

But Irwin was.

"So I guess you need to pick which is more important to you," he told her. "The CrimeBiters or other stuff."

Daisy turned bright red. "We're not even officially a gang right now."

"I only took up lacrosse because you said you'd come to all the games," I reminded her. "And you've barely come to any."

"You guys are putting too much pressure on me!" Daisy snapped. "I should be able to have a life, you know! And sometimes that life is outside the CrimeBiters!" She flashed her eyes at me and Baxter. "You two are busy with lacrosse, you should know that better than anyone!"

"Uh—" I said, but Daisy wasn't finished.

"If you guys can't handle me having a life, then I'm sorry, but we can't be friends." Then she stormed back to her table, leaving us standing there with our mouths open.

"Who needs her!" Irwin said finally. Then he winced in pain. "I have a stomachache all of a sudden. I think I need to go to the nurse's office."

He ran out of the cafeteria.

And just like that, we'd broken up again. It was the shortest reunion in history.

I looked at Baxter.

"See you tonight at the game," he said.

CHAPTER 30

WE WERE PLAYING THE CHAMPIONSHIP FINAL at the high school, and it was our only night game of the season. That meant two things:

(1) There wouldn't be any injuries caused by our lousy field.

(2) Abby, who loved nighttime, would be all hyped up.

"Are you sure we should take her?" my mom asked my dad as we were leaving the house. "I'm not so sure it's a good idea."

"You said!" I insisted. "You can't change your minds now!"

My dad, who cared way more about the game than I did (not that he would ever admit it), looked worried that I would become distracted and upset. "Let's just do it for Jimmy," he told my mom. "It's fine. I'll hold her. Mrs. Cragg can help us too."

I stopped walking. "Mrs. Cragg is coming?"

"Yup," my dad said. "She wanted to watch you and Baxter play."

I smiled inside. "Cool."

I had to get there early for warm-ups, so once we got there my dad decided to try and tire Abby out before the game started.

"I'll take her for a nice long run," he said.

"Sounds good, Dad. I have to go."

I started to run away when my dad said, "Jimmy."

I turned back. "Yeah, Dad?"

"About Abby . . ." he said, but then just shook his head.

"Dad, it's okay. We'll figure it out after the game, okay?"

He looked like he was about to say something, then changed his mind.

"Okay, son. Good luck."

"Thanks, Dad."

I ran off to join my teammates, who were gathering by the bench.

"Yo, Jimmy!" Chad said, coming up to me and giving me a big high five. He was on crutches, so obviously he wasn't going to be playing. "You get a good night's sleep? You're going to need to be wide awake out there today."

I nodded and started putting my stuff on. I didn't feel much like talking. I just wanted to have a good game, since it was pretty much the only thing in my life that was going well right about then.

After a few minutes, Baxter pointed across the field. "Hey, Jimmy, isn't that your dad with Abby? She's playing with some dog who's, like, three times as big as she is!"

I turned and saw Abby and my dad at the far end of the field, by the track. She was jumping on top of a Saint Bernard. A Saint Bernard I recognized.

Coach Knight came up to me. "Jimmy, please go tell your dad he's not allowed to walk his dog on the field," he said. "And be quick about it."

"Got it," I said.

I ran over, and sure enough, it was Thor. I had no idea what he was doing there. Some man I'd never seen before was walking him. Abby, meanwhile, was jumping up and down on Thor's back, with my dad holding on to her leash for dear life.

"This big dog has the patience of a saint," my dad said.

"Well, he is a Saint Bernard," I said. Then I looked at the man. "Are you friends with Mr. Swab? Why are you here with Thor?"

"I work for Coach Swab," the man said. He nodded down at the two dogs. "He says Thor is his good-luck charm."

"*Coach* Swab?" I asked, shocked.

The guy nodded. "Yeah, Ned Swab. The coach of LaxMax."

"Wait a second," I said. "Are you serious? Mr. Swab is the coach of LaxMax?"

"You're darn right I'm serious," the guy said. "But not half as serious as Coach Swab. That man doesn't kid around. He'll stop at nothing to win." He pointed up the hill. "Look, here he comes now."

I followed his gaze to the parking lot and saw two giant luxury buses pulling in. They both said LAXMAX on the side.

FACT: It's never a good sign when the opposing team has buses nicer than the pros.

My dad whistled. "Whoa."

"Like I said, he doesn't kid around," the guy said.

Kids started piling out of the buses. It seemed like there were zillions of them, and they were all giant.

"Jeez," I said.

The man smiled. "Yeah. Jeez just about sums it up."

Mr. Swab was the last one off the second bus. He saw us, walked over, and shook the guy's hand. "Can you make sure all the water gets to the sidelines, Jeff?" he said.

The man named Jeff nodded. "I'm on it, sir."

Mr. Swab turned to me and frowned. "Jimmy! What are you doing here?"

"I'm the goalie for Quietville," I told him.

"No kidding! You're the kid Bill Knight has been telling me about? What do you know!" He looked at me intently. "Well, maybe we'll see you on our LaxMax squad next year. In the meantime, be careful out there today. We got some big boys on our team."

"I will, sir," I said. "I'm confused, though. I thought you were a businessman."

"I am," said Mr. Swab. "I'm in the winning business."

"Is it true your team hasn't lost a game in six years?" my dad asked Mr. Swab.

"That's right," Mr. Swab answered. "At LaxMax, we're built for success. And with our brand-new facilities and some new coaching techniques, we're going to be successful for a long time to come."

"What about all the other lacrosse programs around here?" asked my dad. "Like the team my son is currently on? What happens to them?"

"Well, that's a good question," Mr. Swab said. "I know you've been having a lot of problems with that field. And as you know, Coach Knight is coming over to our program next year. But there are plenty of programs for kids who want to participate at a less competitive level. We compete at an elite level."

My dad scratched his head. "Aren't these kids a little young to be worried about elite levels?"

"Sports is about being the best, no matter what age you are," Mr. Swab said. "Our goal is to make sure boys like your son here join our program. That's what it takes to be the gold standard of lacrosse in this whole area." He looked down at Abby, who was looking up at Mr. Swab suspiciously. "Has she settled down since last night?"

"Again, I'm really sorry," my dad said. "We are figuring out what to do with her."

"Well, I hope so," Mr. Swab said. "We can't have dangerous animals running free now, can we?"

"Abby never growls at somebody unless it's for a good reason," I said.

My dad looked horrified. "Jimmy!"

Mr. Swab laughed. "No, no, it's okay," he said. "If there's one thing I've learned in this world, it's that you can't make friends with everybody."

"I suppose that's true," said my dad.

Mr. Swab nodded in the direction of his team. "Well, time to get on with it. Good luck today, son."

As Mr. Swab walked away, I saw my dad looking at him with a weird expression on his face. It was like he was jealous, impressed, and annoyed, all at the same time.

"He's not so great," I said to my dad.

"Try telling him that," my dad answered.

CHAPTER 31

AFTER TWO MINUTES, we were already losing, 3–0.

"Jimmy!" hollered Coach Knight. "Get your head in the game!"

My head's not the problem, I wanted to holler back. The problem was that we stank compared to LaxMax, especially since we didn't have Chad. They were bigger, faster, quicker, and stronger, not to mention the fact that they had *way* fancier uniforms than we did.

After their second goal, the kid who scored ran by me and said, "You're the kid who's supposed to join our team next year? Show us what you got."

By the end of the first quarter, it was 5–0.

We ran to the sideline.

"Guys!" Coach said. "Guys! Guys! Guys!"

The team stood there, waiting for him to come up with a second word.

"Guys! You're playing scared! They're good, but they're not gods. They're boys, just like you!"

"They might be boys," Baxter mumbled, "but they're not just like us."

At the beginning of the second quarter, our team manager, Mikey Parker, was running off the field after a water break when he tripped on our sideline and skinned his elbow. My first thought was *Here we go again!*—but then I remembered we were playing at the high school.

"You know it's not a good sign when someone on your team gets injured and they're not even playing," I said. I was standing by myself in the goal, though, so no one heard it.

Then, with three minutes left in the first half, we scored. And wouldn't you know it, it was an amazing play by Baxter that made it happen. He received a pass at the halfway line, faked out three guys, then shot with his left hand, even though he's a righty.

Suddenly, we were only behind 8–1!

FACT: Sometimes, the score doesn't matter. Unfortunately, this was not one of those times.

Okay, so it's not exactly like we were right back in the game, but it was something to get excited about, right? So we got excited. I hooted and hollered from my lonely spot in the goal, while Baxter ran over to the sideline to slap hands with all our teammates.

He was halfway down the high-five line when I saw him suddenly crumple to the ground and let out a piercing scream. It was so loud that I could hear it all the way across the field.

The whole place went silent as Coach Knight went over to Baxter and helped him to the bench. I saw Baxter's mom come down from the crowd and push her way through to try to console him. He was crying.

"What happened?" I kept repeating to anyone on the field who would listen. "What happened?"

"I think he fell and hurt his foot or something," said a LaxMax kid. "Bummer. It was a nice goal."

After another minute, everyone was ready to start the game again, but something just didn't feel right. I went over it in my head: Kids had been getting injured all season long. Then, yesterday at practice, two more kids got hurt. Today during the game, two more kids.

I didn't care what field we were playing on—something weird was going on.

I thought about what Mrs. Cragg had said: *It almost sounds like someone is doing it on purpose.*

And then I thought about what Shep had said at the first obedience class: *When something happens often enough, it becomes more than a coincidence. It becomes a pattern.*

Suddenly I found myself running off the field.

I heard voices aimed in my direction.

"Hey!"

"Where are you going?"

"What's happening?"

"Come on, kid, the game's about to start again!"

Coach Knight saw me coming and ran out onto the field to meet me. He was smiling, trying to stay positive. "Jimmy, what's up? We just scored! Come on, we can come back! I need you out there!"

"Is Baxter okay?"

"He'll be fine! Just a little knee sprain. Good as new in a few weeks." Coach tapped me on the helmet, expecting me to turn around and run back to my position.

But I just stayed there. His smile disappeared. "Jimmy, are you serious? Let's go. Now."

"Too many people are getting hurt. It's been going on the whole season."

He pulled me aside, where no one could hear us. "Jimmy. I get it. But you have to realize, that's sports. People get injured. Even kids sometimes. Everyone gets knocked down in life. It's learning how to get back up that defines us as boys . . . and men."

I looked at him. That was a great speech, but he was missing the point.

"Too many people are getting hurt," I repeated. "And I think it's because someone wants them to get hurt."

Coach Knight looked at me like I had two heads. "Huh?"

I turned around and ran to the center of the field, where the face-offs take place after every goal.

"Somebody is after us!" I shouted, loud enough so the people in the crowd could hear me too. "We've had eleven kids injured this year, including four in the last two days! Somebody is trying to hurt us!"

Everyone started murmuring. I couldn't quite hear what they were saying, but I'm pretty sure it was along the lines of *This kid is crazy.*

"Play the game!" hollered someone from the LaxMax side of the crowd.

"Man up!" yelled someone else.

But I wouldn't budge.

As people got more confused, I saw my family in the crowd. My parents were making their way down to the field, trying to figure out what was going on, so they'd given Abby's leash to Mrs. Cragg. She saw me and yelled, "Good for you!" then gave me two thumbs-up.

Oops.

FACT: Never give someone two thumbs-up when you're holding a hyperactive dog on a leash.

Mrs. Cragg dropped the leash for a second, and that was all Abby needed.

In a flash, she leapt over about four rows of people (remember I said she could fly?), easily cleared a four-foot-high fence (the flying thing again), and bolted onto the field, where she came running up to me and started jumping up and down.

"Not now, girl," I said. "Not now! Stop jumping!"

She did stop jumping—but only because she was ready for her next activity, which was to run giant circles around me. After the first two circles, the other kids on the field started laughing, but the adults weren't amused. First I refuse to keep playing, then my dog decides to make the field her own personal playground. This was not the way the championship game was supposed to go.

Another dog started barking, and everyone perked their ears up, Abby included. The barking was coming from the LaxMax side of the field.

I knew who it was, and so did Abby.

She sprinted over to the LaxMax sideline and barged her way through the crowd until she found Thor, who was tied to the bleachers. It was the happiest reunion you've ever seen, even though they'd seen each other approximately twenty-five minutes earlier. Abby was running around Thor, who had managed to free himself from his leash and was chasing Abby.

Mr. Swab was hollering, "Get off the field now!"

My dad had reached us too, and he was hollering at Mr. Swab.

"How dare you talk to my son that way!"

"I'm not talking to your son!" Mr. Swab yelled back. "I'm talking to the dogs!"

Coach Knight was standing between them. "Let's just call an early halftime and get this sorted out," he said, but no one was listening to him. My mom was there too, and some other parents, and soon a bunch of adults were screaming at each other, even though no one appeared to be listening to anything anyone else was saying.

Abby and Thor, meanwhile, had begun their favorite activity of all time: digging holes. And as it turned out, a lacrosse field is the perfect place to dig holes.

As I watched them dig, an idea started forming in my head.

Hey, I thought.

Wait a second.

CHAPTER 32

WITHOUT ANOTHER WORD, I hustled back to our sideline. As I ran, I thought about the four kids who'd fallen and hurt themselves over the last two days. They'd all fallen right near our bench!

I ran over to Mikey Parker, who was standing on the sideline with a bandage on his elbow. "Can you show me exactly where you got hurt?"

He scratched his head, confused. "Huh?"

"Where you got hurt! Show me!"

"Oh. Uh, sure." He walked over to a spot near the bench. "It was somewhere around here."

I kneeled down and felt on the ground. Sure enough, there was a hole. It was surrounded by dirt and covered up by cut grass, so it was hard to see, but there was definitely a hole. Which looked a lot like a hole a dog might dig.

I ran over to Baxter, who was still icing his ankle. "Baxter! Where did you fall?"

He scowled at me. "How am I supposed to know?"

"Try to remember!" I hollered, then remembered he was in pain. "Please," I added.

He moaned and rolled his eyes, but he pointed to a spot on our sideline. "I came off the field around there." I ran over to the spot and knelt down on the ground. And again, there was another hole—just as hard to spot as the last one, but unmistakable.

Suddenly I heard someone yelling my name. "Jimmy! Jimmy!" I turned around and saw a familiar face sprinting toward me. He was wearing his CrimeBiters sweatshirt.

It was Irwin.

"No way!" I said. "What are you doing here? What are you doing on the field?"

Irwin shrugged like it was no big deal. "It seemed like you needed help."

I suddenly felt incredibly grateful. "I do."

Irwin held up a small blue dog tag that said NORTH-PORT ARF! on it. "Look what I found!" he said. "I found it over by one of the holes near the benches. Isn't that where Abby went to obedience training?"

I turned the tag over and read the back. CONGRATU-
LATIONS THOR—YOU'RE AN ARFULLY GOOD DOG!

It must have fallen off his collar.

That was all the proof I needed.

Suddenly everything made sense. The open drain
pipe on the field. The broken bench. The sprinklers. The
holes on the sideline.

I ran back out onto the middle of the field and started
yelling.

"I know what happened!"

Everyone looked up from their arguing.

"I know what happened here! I know why kids on our
team are getting hurt! I know why kids have been getting
hurt all season!"

Everyone started walking toward me. The first person
to reach me was the man who had been walking Thor
before the game.

"You better watch yourself, son," he hissed at me.
"Making false accusations can get you in big trouble."

The man was just about to stick a finger in my face
when a noise stopped him.

"GRRROOOWWWWWL!"

I looked down and there was Abby, standing next to

me, walking slowly toward the man. Then she took a glance up at me, as if to say, *I'm back.*

FACT: Sometimes, the growl of a dog is the best sound in the world.

The man started backing up slowly. "Get that thing away from me."

"Not until you tell everyone what happened here," I said.

"I don't know what you're talking about," the man said.

My parents came running up to me, and Mrs. Cragg grabbed Abby and put her back on the leash.

"Jimmy!" cried my mom. "What is going on here? Did this man do something to you?"

"That's what I'm trying to find out," I said.

"Where's Mr. Swab?" I yelled. My eyes searched all over the place, until they landed back on the man. "WHERE'S YOUR BOSS?" I took the leash from Mrs. Cragg and pointed at Abby, who was staring at the man, fangs and all. "If you don't tell me now, Abby will make you."

A look of panic crossed the guy's face. "I don't know! I just did what he told me to do. It's not my fault!"

Everyone gasped. "What's this guy talking about?" my dad said.

But I didn't answer him, because I was looking around, all over the field, and slowly realizing something.

Necks craned, heads turned, eyes searched—and everyone else realized it too.

Mr. Swab was nowhere in sight.

CHAPTER 33

"FIND MR. SWAB!"

As soon as the cry went up, Abby and I started sprinting up to the parking lot.

After ten more steps, I noticed someone on my right side.

"I'm with you all the way," Irwin said.

"Let's get this guy," I said.

He nodded, trying to keep up. Irwin wasn't exactly in the best shape. He was pretty much in the same shape I was in, before I started playing lacrosse.

"I didn't even know you were coming today!" I told him.

Irwin tried to talk and pant at the same time. "I . . . wanted . . . to . . . see . . . the game."

I stopped for just a second so he could catch his breath.

"You don't have to do this if you don't want to," I told him.

He bent over, grabbing his knees, then looked back up at me. "You think I'd miss all this excitement?" he asked. "Besides, we're a gang, aren't we?"

I felt a warm feeling in my chest. "Yeah, we are."

We took off again, the three of us, Irwin, Abby, and me, with about twenty adults (including my parents) close behind. We scrambled up the hill, ran across the basketball courts, and got to the parking lot, where I stopped dead in my tracks.

Daisy, of all people, was walking straight toward us.

"Hey," she said to us, a little nervously. "What's going on? Why are you guys up here? Isn't the game still going on?"

"It's a long story," I said. "What are you doing here?"

She looked down. "You were right, Jimmy," she said. "I made a promise to come to the games, and I let you down. So here I am." She smiled. "I'm sorry I'm late."

My heart flooded with happiness. "No need to apologize!" I said, trying to sound casual. "Thanks for coming." I was just about to get totally distracted by that whole topic, but by some miracle I managed to remember why I'd run up to the parking lot. "Hey, have you seen a man go by, probably looked like he was in a big hurry?"

Daisy nodded. "You mean him?" She pointed across the lot to where Mr. Swab was loading Thor into a giant SUV.

"Hey!" I yelled. "You're supposed to be a big-shot sports coach and you're running away from a couple of kids?"

Mr. Swab turned and looked at us angrily. "I'm not running away!" he sputtered. "This has turned into a charade! I want no part of it! This is a disgrace to elite competitive sports everywhere!"

"Stop right there!" Irwin yelled. "In the name of the CrimeBiters!"

Daisy and I looked at him.

"Worth a shot," he said, shrugging.

Mr. Swab ignored Irwin and managed to get Thor in the car (no easy task when you're talking about a 150-pound Saint Bernard) and shut the door, but he made one key mistake: He left the window open.

FACT: There aren't too many things Abby likes more than an open car window. (Just ask Barnaby Bratford.)

WHOOSH!

As Mr. Swab tried to pull out of his parking space,

Abby flew into the open window and landed right on Thor's head. Thor was thrilled to see her, and their third happy reunion in less than an hour took place in the backseat of Mr. Swab's car.

FACT: Dogs love reunions almost as much as they love food.

After about ten seconds, Thor and Abby realized the backseat wasn't quite big enough for their shenanigans, and they tumbled into the *front* seat of Mr. Swab's car. Which was bad for Mr. Swab, who was busy trying to navigate a tight turn.

"Get off me, dogs!" he yelled, but Thor must have thought that was part of a game, because he started licking Mr. Swab all over his face.

FACT: It's hard to steer a car when a giant dog is licking you all over your face.

Mr. Swab proceeded to crash his car directly into a sign that said CAUTION! SCHOOLCHILDREN.

"Argggggghhhh!" he screamed, which we could hear loud and clear, since the window was open.

By now, there were a ton of people in the parking lot. Irwin, Daisy, and me; my parents, my sister, and Mrs. Cragg; Coach Knight; a bunch of parents and kids from both teams; and people who were just watching the game.

Altogether there were about fifty of us, and we had Mr. Swab trapped.

"Sir, you're surrounded," I said, in my best *STOP! POLICE!* voice. "Please step out of the car."

At least Abby listened to me. She hopped out the back window and jumped into my arms.

"Hey, girl," I whispered, nuzzling her ear. "Good job."

Thanks, she said, even though she didn't actually say it.

The front door of the SUV suddenly opened, and in a flash Mr. Swab stomped over in my direction, wagging his finger. "You've got this all wrong!" he hollered. Unfortunately for him, he only got about three steps before Daisy stuck her foot out and tripped him, sending him sprawling to the ground.

"My knee!" Mr. Swab howled. "I think I hurt my knee!"

"Suck it up," muttered Chad Knight, who proceeded to use one of his crutches to pin Mr. Swab down.

"Tell everyone what happened," I told him. "Tell everyone what you did."

"I don't know what you're talking about!" he gasped.

"Fine, then I'll tell them," I said. I raised my voice so everyone could hear me. "You planned this whole thing from the beginning because you were worried that we would beat you and ruin your precious LaxMax perfect record," I said. "And you used your awesome dog, Thor, to do all your dirty work for you."

Everyone looked at Thor, who was wagging his tail happily.

FACT: Sometimes the less dogs know, the better.

"You didn't think you'd get caught because everybody already thought our field was so terrible," I explained.

Coach Knight looked shocked. "Is this true, Ned?" he asked his friend.

Mr. Swab shrugged. "The field *is* terrible," he mumbled.

I went on. "You must have snuck over to our field with poor Thor the night before the Northport game. Then you had Thor take the top off of the drain pipe, just like the Drag and Drop exercise that Shep taught us."

"That's ridiculous," Mr. Swab claimed.

I ignored him. "And you wrapped bacon around the legs of the bench so Thor would gnaw them off, like he did during the Just Chew It exercise."

"Absurd," he insisted.

I forged ahead. "You had Thor play Bury the Bone by digging holes on our sideline, yesterday at practice and today at the game. All so kids on our team would get hurt, and you could win the championship."

"Preposterous," he muttered, a little less forcefully.

"This is the most despicable thing I've ever heard," muttered my mom.

"If it's true," added my dad.

"And somehow you had Thor chew a hole in poor Kyle Shuken's stick!" I yelled, my voice rising.

"THAT ONE'S NOT TRUE!" Mr. Swab wailed. "I NEVER DID THAT!"

Everyone stopped murmuring and stared at him.

He said he didn't do *that* one.

Which meant he did the *other* ones.

When Mr. Swab realized what he'd done, his shoulders slumped. "Okay, fine. Maybe I did have Thor take the drainpipe cover. I thought maybe one or two kids might sprain an ankle, and your team wouldn't be as good. I figured that would be the end of it. But then you started winning and you kept winning! So I had to keep going! I couldn't lose the championship this year! Not when we're about to build a big new facility that will be the best in the whole state!"

"You're a disgrace, Ned," said Coach Knight, shaking his head. "I believed in you. But you're nothing but a sneaky, no-good cheater."

"He's worse than that," I said. "He's a criminal."

"If I lost the championship, then my whole dream would go up in smoke!" Mr. Swab sputtered. "I can't lose.

Everything would be ruined! My business, my perfect record, my reputation for being the best! Everything!"

I smiled. "Like I once heard you say, it's a doggy dog world, right, Mr. Swab?"

He looked at me like I was the gum that got stuck to the bottom of his shoe. "That's *dog-eat-dog*, you little twerp. Don't you know anything?"

FACT: "Doggy dog world" is a much nicer phrase than "dog-eat-dog world."

"I know one thing," I said. "We win the game by forfeit."

CHAPTER 34

TEN MINUTES LATER, the police were there, taking statements from everybody in the parking lot. Eventually, they took Mr. Swab away for questioning.

Everyone was finally starting to drift away when another police car pulled into the parking lot.

"Oh boy," my mom said. "Hasn't there been enough excitement for one day?"

A cop got out and said, "We've got a problem." Then he pointed to his backseat. "Does anyone know whose dog this is? I found him wandering out in the street."

"Thor!" I yelled. There he was, the big Saint Bernard, hanging out in the backseat of a police car. Somehow, in all the commotion, he must have slipped away.

"Is he your dog?" the cop asked me.

I stared up at my parents. "Can we take him? Can we? Can we?"

"Since you asked me three times, I'll answer you three times," my mom said. "No, no, and no."

"But we have to!"

"One crazy hound in the house is enough," my dad said. "Sorry."

"He's Mr. Swab's dog!" someone shouted. The policeman shrugged and said, "Okay. I guess I'll take him downtown and we'll figure it out there."

He started to get back into the car when a voice rang out. "I'll take him!"

Everyone looked to see who was volunteering to take a 150-pound, drooling, shedding beast.

Mrs. Cragg stepped forward.

"I could use a friend," she said. "And I bet he could too. If for some reason he might need to find another home, then I'd like to have him."

Thor leapt out of the car, said hi to Abby, and then gave Mrs. Cragg a big lick on the face.

My mom shook her head in disbelief.

"Now I've seen it all," she said.

CHAPTER 35

AS WE ALL STARTED TO WALK BACK DOWN THE HILL to get our lacrosse stuff, I noticed something.

Daisy wasn't moving.

"Are you coming?" I said.

"Yeah, Daisy, come on," Irwin added.

But she stood there. "I'm not sure."

Irwin and I looked at each other, and both decided the same thing at the same time.

"The gang is back together," I said. "For good this time. And that includes you."

"If you *want* to come back," Irwin said.

After a beat, I added, "And Mara can join too."

"Oh, Mara," Daisy said. "Don't worry about her. It turns out she's in the Quietville Bagpiping Club, so she's probably too busy to join."

Yes! I thought. Then I remembered that Jonny Galt,

the kid who used to play goalie, quit lacrosse for the same reason. Jeez, who knew bagpiping was so popular?

"HEY, GUYS!" a voice called.

We stared and saw somebody walking up toward us. He was going really slowly, and as he got closer, I could tell he was walking on crutches.

We all squinted. "Who is that?" Irwin said.

After a few more seconds, I could tell who it was.

"It's Baxter!" I exclaimed.

We ran down to greet him. "Are you okay?" we all said.

He nodded, but I could tell he was in pain. "Yeah. I was getting ice on my knee. I heard I missed all the excitement."

"You sure did!" I launched into a play-by-play description of everything that happened, but Baxter stopped me after four words.

"Can you just wait a second?" He turned to Daisy. "Did you guys all make up?"

We all nodded.

"Well, that's good," Baxter said. "Daisy is awesome and smart. But sometimes it seems like all you guys do is fight over her. And that's not fair."

Irwin looked at me. "We promise not to act all crazy if Daisy wants to have a friend outside the gang, right, Jimmy?"

"Right," I said.

Daisy grinned. "And Irwin and I promise we won't go off and do things by ourselves just because you two are busy with sports or something else, right, Irwin?"

"Right," Irwin said. "And I also promise to treat Baxter like a full member of the club."

"Thanks," Baxter said. "And I promise not to be jealous just because Jimmy is, like, the best lacrosse player ever."

"I wouldn't go *that* far," Irwin said, but he was smiling when he said it.

"Then it's settled!" Daisy said happily. "No more arguing about silly stuff!"

"We've got way more important things to do, anyway," I added. "We're the CrimeBiters."

"The CrimeBiters!" Irwin said.

"The CrimeBiters!" Baxter joined in.

We all formed a circle and put our hands into the middle.

"CRIMEBITERS FOREVER!" we all yelled.

As we all walked down the hill, I looked down at Abby.

"What's that, girl? You think we should go get ice cream? Great idea!"

She barked, and the whole gang laughed.

"Okay, now I'm finally convinced," Irwin said. "She's a superdog after all!"

EPILOGUE

NED SWAB WAS CHARGED with endangering the welfare of children, and was released on bail to await trial. Meanwhile, Irwin made the fascinating discovery that if you mix up the letters of his name, they spell BAD NEWS.

LaxMax was disbanded as a program, but most of the players on the team joined a new program called LaxPro, which is just as intense and time-consuming as LaxMax. Jimmy, however, decided to stay with the Quietville team, because it's a lot more fun.

After **Mr. Swab** decided he didn't want Thor anymore, **Mrs. Cragg** was able to adopt him. They have become best friends, even though Mrs. Cragg's house is a mess and her yard looks like the surface of the moon.

Chad Knight decided that sports were too dangerous, so he's taken up ballroom dancing. He's on the way to becoming a nationally ranked dancer in his age group.

Coach Knight was dead set against the whole ballroom dancing thing at first, but once he saw his son do the tango, he couldn't stop bragging about it. He wanted to coach dancing too, until he found out there was a strict no-whistle policy.

Shep has expanded his dog obedience program to include a new class, Dogs Rock: How Music Can Soothe Your Beast's Savage Soul. Jimmy and Abby continue to visit Shep at the shelter once a week, so Abby can practice following her star.

The CrimeBiters continue to meet regularly at the clubhouse, awaiting their next opportunity to fight crime. And Abby hasn't eaten a shoe in months! As far as we know.

STAY TUNED FOR

CRIME BITERS!

DOG DAY AFTER SCHOOL

ACKNOWLEDGMENTS

THANKS TO MY WIFE, Cathy, for letting me keep Abby even though she's a total handful; my kids, Charlie, Joe, and Jack, for teaching me about the bond between children and dogs; my dogs, Coco and Abby, for being nonstop sources of pleasure (except when they're nightmares); and my editor, Nancy, for letting me write books about Cathy, Charlie, Joe, Jack, Coco, and Abby.

ABOUT THE AUTHOR

TOMMY GREENWALD AND HIS DOG, ABBY

TOMMY GREENWALD is the author of the first book in the CrimeBiters! series, *My Dog is Better than Your Dog*, and the Charlie Joe Jackson series about the most reluctant reader ever born. Tommy lives in Connecticut with his wife, Cathy; their kids, Charlie, Joe, and Jack; and their dogs, Coco and Abby. Abby is not necessarily a crime-fighting vampire dog—but she makes Tommy and his family very, very happy, which is definitely a kind of superpower when you think about it.